ONCE IN THE BLUE MOON

Once in the Blue Moon

VIRGINIA MILLER REEVES

ILLUSTRATED BY KYLE HOBRATSCHK

DEEP VELLUM PUBLISHING
DALLAS, TEXAS

Deep Vellum Publishing
3000 Commerce Street, Dallas, Texas 75226
deepvellum.org · @deepvellum

Deep Vellum is a 501c3 nonprofit literary arts organization
founded in 2013 with the mission to bring
the world into conversation through literature.

Support for this publication has been provided in part by grants from the National
Endowment for the Arts, the Texas Commission on the Arts, the City of Dallas
Office of Arts and Culture, the Communities Foundation of Texas, and the
George and Fay Young Foundation.

LIBRARY OF CONGRESS CATALOGING-IN-PUBLICATION DATA

Names: Reeves, Virginia Miller, author.

Title: Once in the Blue Moon / Virginia Miller Reeves.

Description: First edition. | Dallas, Texas : Deep Vellum Publishing, 2024.

Identifiers: LCCN 2023039370 (print) | LCCN 2023039371 (ebook) | ISBN
9781646053025 (hardcover) | ISBN 9781646053179 (ebook)

Subjects: LCSH: Rural families--Oklahoma--Fiction. | Farm
life--Oklahoma--Fiction. | LCGFT: Domestic fiction. | Novels.

Classification: LCC PS3618.E44583 O53 2024 (print) | LCC PS3618.E44583
(ebook) | DDC 813/.6--dc23/eng/20231010

LC record available at https://lccn.loc.gov/2023039370

LC ebook record available at https://lccn.loc.gov/2023039371

ISBN (hardcover) 978-1-64605-302-5 | ISBN (Ebook) 978-1-64605-317-9

Cover illustration by Kyle Hobratschk

Cover design by Andy Anzollitto

Interior layout and typesetting by KGT

PRINTED IN CANADA

For my sisters Frances and Gloria

"You must do the thing you think you cannot do."
—Eleanor Roosevelt

AUTHOR'S NOTE

I learned the alphabet by the dim light of an oil lamp in a kitchen heated by a woodstove burning sweet cedar. My eldest sister taught me to read long before I started to school. I remember her saying, "You are way ahead of yourself." We had no telephone. We had no electricity. But we had dreams.

Daddy had lost his dreams somewhere in the midst of the Dust Bowl, the Great Depression, and World War II. It seemed he had a secret suffering we could not understand. He blamed himself for being broke . . . he never blamed the difficult times or limited opportunities. He felt at fault: he couldn't see any future. It was an open wound that he began filling with whiskey.

In that same kitchen, I learned that what you know and what you feel are very different. Terror is something you feel. When you worry over losing everything you love, especially family, what you feel is stark terror. The thin edge of poverty can cut both ways. It can kill you— or cause you to rise up and seize the chance for change.

There is an enduring valuable lesson in not giving up. You may find it difficult to believe that a skinny young girl could actually live this story. It didn't seem unusual then, but I will say it didn't happen to just anyone. It happened to me. Let me tell you.

ONCE IN THE BLUE MOON

PROLOGUE

I KEPT WATCH OVER THE whole room from my perch. Mama claimed this is the biggest and nicest kitchen we've ever had, and like her, I hope we never have to leave it. Lately, I'm scared we might lose it, might lose everything, if things don't change. I'm worried about Daddy. When he smiles, a dark room lights up like the noonday sun, but when he's drinking, it's as if we're in a terrible storm. And these days he's drinking a lot of whiskey and acting like a crazy person. Why can't he be like he was before?

The kitchen felt warm when I was on my bench behind the woodstove. I scooted the bench so close to the stove that I almost cooked my front side. When I turned to bake my back, I was careful not to burn my elbows like before. My scars, healed now, still smelled of the burn cream Dr. Haas sent from town.

My sisters' faces shone above their books and papers as they did their homework in the dim light of the oil lamp. They seemed separated from the rest of the dark room. I mustn't say a word out loud, Mama said. Mama stayed quiet too. She stitched quilt squares, moving her rocker to the beat of the slapping porch curtains as the wind sucked them back and forth.

The wood fell and shifted in the stove. It was a lonely sound, reminding me that Daddy was out there, alone, on this black night. I hoped he would come home and bring what I need. I peered out the window, then with my finger wrote the word *Daddy* on the frosted glass. That way, I could watch for Daddy's truck lights as I practice my writing. Lately, I've had a lot of practice. How many nights have I waited?

When I saw the circles of light come over the far hill, I crossed my fingers. Maybe this time he remembered. Mrs. Goggins said I needed my own and Mama promised.

He pulled the truck right up beside the house instead of putting it in the shed. We heard him singing and laughing even before he burst through the back doorway. I hurried to my bench as his loud voice bellowed out a verse from "The Old Rugged Cross."

He laughed and staggered around the room,

knocking into the table. I'd seen him act like this before. My sister says he goes to the Blue Moon and drinks too much. Mama stood steadying him, and guided him into his oak rocker, still in his wool topcoat and crumpled hat. He was "too big" again.

I leaned out from my perch and caught his grinning blue eyes fastened on me. He fumbled in his pocket, and then tossed me a brown sack covered with the sharp odor of whiskey. I peeked inside. It was red. Smiling, I showed it to Mama and my sisters. It was red and brand-new. No one had a red pencil. Even Mrs. Goggins's pencil was black. At last, I had my own. And it was red.

He motioned me to give it back to him so he could sharpen it with his pocketknife. As he began, I saw he could not cut it right. Lost in song, he paused just long enough to dig deep creases in the arms of the rocking chair. Then, I watched every sharp down cut as more and more tiny bits of red flew away. He was cutting so much. He was cutting too much! My pencil was disappearing. He couldn't stop his whittling any more than he could stop his singing or drinking.

I could barely breathe when he handed it back to me. I placed what was left on the bench next to me and measured it. My beautiful tall red pencil was as short and puny as my smallest finger.

I glanced at Mama and my sisters, then at the word "Daddy" fading on the frosted windowpane before I moved to hide behind the big black woodstove. Hurt and disappointment brought stinging tears to my eyes.

He will not see me cry, I vowed.

ONE

WILEY'S SILKY VOICE AND JANGLING guitar rang clear in the bacon-scented hubbub of our kitchen, the station tuned to WKY in Oklahoma City. The Truetone radio, wired to an automobile battery on the floor under the buffet, gave us some lively music on this freezing January morning.

"This old radio is the best thing we own. But I sure wish electricity would come out to the farms," I said.

"Just give it more time, Maggie. I bet when this war is over, we'll get electricity," Mama said.

"I'll probably be all grown-up by then," I grumbled.

"You wait and see. I think the war will end this year. Then good times will come for everyone." She paused, glancing through the window. "Looks like snow. Better bundle up and get going."

"I can't fasten my boots," I whined, after my third try. Mama leaned over and quickly snapped them shut making sure my leggings were tucked tightly into what she called my galoshes.

"In the Oklahoma hills where I was born . . ." Celia sang along with the radio music. She seemed exceptionally happy, even volunteering, "I'll carry your dinner bucket, Maggie."

Celia was older than me and her brown-black eyes were just like Mama's and Great-Grandmother Caroline Pate's. She could already drive the tractor and milk the cows. It was clear her heart, like mine, belonged to Daddy. Celia always defended Daddy whenever Sarah was angry with him, which lately was a lot. Celia pretended happiness better than anyone I knew.

I grinned at her. Now, if Daddy went with us, I could help with the lantern. But some mornings, he just stayed in the rocker staring into space, his energy and good nature drained. On those mornings, I worried, and agreed with Sarah when she complained, "If Mama doesn't do something soon to stop his drinking, we'll lose this place."

But Daddy was putting on his overcoat and cap! He *was* coming with us, even after the terrible night before.

As we were leaving the warm kitchen, the

announcer ended the program with his usual "aw-re-vore." It was his Oklahoma version of the fancy French "au revoir" and hearing it meant we were right on time to head for our bus. On days when the radio battery was dead and the radio silent, we said it for him. Mostly though, we said it for ourselves. Farewell until another morning in this kitchen—until tomorrow morning, and hopefully every day thereafter.

It was still a night sky. The lantern's glow lighted our little procession, guiding us to the red dirt road. Looking back at the house, I saw Teddy run under my rope swing in the cedar thicket, setting it in motion as if it were a summer day.

I waved goodbye to the windmill. It was a tall skel-eton guarding the house and the barnyard. In warm weather I climbed to the top to look out over our fields and pastures. No matter where I looked, the horizon was flat red dirt, except below the barn where trees bor-dered our creek. Some people said: Oklahoma, home of the red man and red dirt. Red like my short little pencil that I'd hidden in my keepsake box. I suddenly remem-bered it and hurried to catch the others.

"No wind," said Daddy.

"Doesn't feel so cold when the wind's gone, does it?" Sarah, my oldest sister, added, giving a whistle to Teddy.

Teddy escorted us down the long road to the four

corners each morning and waited until we were inside the yellow school bus before heading home. Mama always said, "I can tell the time of day by Teddy. He leaves the porch at exactly the same time each afternoon to meet the bus and bring you girls home."

Teddy and I usually explored the steep banks alongside the road on our daily jaunts to and from the school bus. Sometimes if I found a treasure—a feather, an odd-shaped rock, a tiny bone, or a bird's nest—I'd keep it in our corner mailbox to be rescued after school.

But the darkness of this winter morning and my itchy wool leggings made any adventure too much work. Even for Teddy. He just trotted beside us, ears pointed, listening, as if guarding our every step.

Celia noticed first. "Snowflakes. Look, it's snowing!"

The flakes were big as nickels. By the time we reached the four corners, the ruts in the road were filled with white. A lone crow cawed deep in the woods, interrupting the stillness. When we saw the headlights from the bus come over the top of the hill, Daddy placed the lantern on top of the row of snow-covered mailboxes and lifted me to blow out the flame.

I gave him the tightest hug I could. A whisker tickle from his handsome face felt somehow reassuring. Most winter days he smelled of coffee, Old Spice, and tobacco. I knew in summer his smell would be completely different: wheat, hay, and his favorite crop, cotton. This morning, Daddy's glistening blue eyes were not like his wild drinking eyes, and his voice was soft and embarrassed. I remembered his sharp, shiny knife cutting into my pencil again and again last night and I shuddered. I was afraid that his weakness, that scary part of him, could ruin everything.

I climbed on board and took a front window seat near Elmer, our driver. As the bus lurched forward, I watched Daddy's lonely silhouette follow Teddy, then disappear into the snowy dark woods of the north pasture.

TWO

I DID NOT WANT TO sing this morning. I leaned against Sarah's safe, warm side. We were both content to let Celia rouse the bus kids in song as only she could do. She organized them in two groups, so they could sing a round, and then she sat facing backward on our bench, her hands directing everyone, as her dark brown hair came flowing out of her wool headscarf.

"She sure loves being in charge," I whispered to Sarah.

"Yes, she's good at it too," Sarah said. Then she asked, "Did you bring your pencil?"

"No. Never! I hid it. I'll never take it to school. The kids would laugh at how stubby it is and they'd laugh at me, too. Never tell, Sarah. Don't tell anyone what happened," I begged.

"Last night seemed like a bad dream," she said hugging me. "It's got to get better."

I nodded. I wanted to believe it would. I looked out the window and watched the swirling snowflakes grow smaller, falling faster and thicker. The trees grew blurry in the falling snow. My head felt blurry too, as I recalled the relentless pencil-whittling, scrape after scrape, until the whole pencil had practically disappeared. Suddenly I was afraid of what else might happen.

I wished I was back at the mailboxes with Daddy and Teddy. I knew that after the bus pulled away, they would cut through the woods and make a jag across the north pasture. If I were with them, Daddy would carry me on his shoulders, and we would laugh as Teddy snooped and sniffed at everything in sight.

I'd hang onto Daddy for dear life and help him believe he could find his old ways today. I'd remind him of when he was fun and easy to love. I'd say, "Daddy, can we play our game? Can you carry two buckets of milk in one hand and me with the other like we used to?" He'd scoop me up, laughing while I giggled and giggled, until he plunked me on the steps to the house next to Mama. Mama would tease, "Arley, you're as strong as Tarzan!" I'd feel how much he loved me, loved us all.

But now I worried he couldn't stop his drinking—no

matter how much I wished he would. I pictured Daddy and Teddy headed to the big barn to begin morning chores. Teddy had been born under the front porch to a stray who left him for Sarah to raise. He'd become a good cattle dog. Daddy appreciated his natural ability. Still, he was never very kind to Teddy. It was clear that Daddy didn't care much for dogs, even if they earned their keep. I loved Teddy, but he was really Sarah's pet. Every day I wished I had an animal of my own. Something that belonged just to me. I seemed to be wishing for a lot of things lately.

As the bus filled with singing and loud laughter, I closed my eyes and pictured Teddy darting under the barnyard fence, barking orders and moving the cows toward the open doorway. They'd follow his commands easily on this cold day. They'd want inside from the wind and snow, but mostly they'd want hay. Good winter grass was scarce.

I thought about Mama and Daddy moving steadily down the long row of munching cows, filling bucket after bucket with streams of warm, white milk. Teddy, resting motionless in the hay, would watch the ratter cats lined up on the loft edge waiting for their pan of creamy milk.

When they were done, Teddy would run ahead to oversee Daddy feeding our huge red bull. Teddy never barked near the bull. He knew not to excite him. He was smart to be afraid of the meanest bull in the entire county. When Grandma Judy-Bob Pate nicknamed our bull "Old Hitler," we had all laughed. But she had just said, "Yessir, he's just like that frightening awful man behind the war in Europe." I thought she was saying the truth because it seemed like everyone was afraid of the real Hitler. Everyone except President Roosevelt and the USA. And for certain, everyone and everything feared our own mean Hitler. Everyone but Daddy.

Beyond the bullpen, Teddy and Daddy would go to the lean-to shed, where the mules, Joe and Slim, waited for breakfast. Joe and Slim had been in our family longer than Sarah, Celia, Teddy, and me. Daddy and the pair had plowed one rent-farm after another, working as a team year after year. When President Roosevelt announced his wartime plan to help farmers supply much-needed wheat and cotton, Mama persuaded Daddy to sign up for the Farm Security Loan. After Mama and Daddy finally got the loan and purchased the noisy Allis-Chalmers tractor, Daddy promised, "The mules will always have a home, no matter what happens."

"Maggie, are you asleep?" Sarah asked, nudging me as the bus swerved.

"No, I was just daydreaming," I answered.

"The storm is getting worse by the minute. I think we should have stayed home today," Sarah said.

"Me too," I mumbled, looking out at the blowing snow. With every sweep of the windshield wipers on the bus, I felt more lonesome for Mama and our cozy kitchen.

As the bus crept through the whiteout, the kids around me grew unusually quiet. Each of us peered out trying to spot the school building. Where was it? We had been on the bus long enough to be near the school.

Finally, as the pattern of the storm quickly shifted, the swirling flakes lessened, and the low-slung brick buildings came into view.

Crossing the frigid playground, I trudged toward the doors to my building as the wind whipped drifts all around me. My footprints quickly disappeared. I struggled and pounded at the heavy doors until Mrs. Goggins finally heard me.

"Maggie, hello, we were worrying about you. Did your bus lose the way?" she asked, "There are not many children as brave as you this morning."

I was glad to see James, my good friend, was already here. After much struggling, I got my leggings, coat, and hat off and onto the cloakroom hook labeled "Maggie Poynter." It was my place.

I loved my schoolroom. I loved the bright colors and the steam radiators: the *entire* room was warm—not like home. Best of all were the electric lights hanging as bright as sunlight over the desks and Mrs. Goggins's big wooden one.

I plopped down and raised my hand asking to borrow a pencil—again. "Please and thank you, Mrs. Goggins."

Someone snickered. I lowered my head, embarrassed that I still didn't have my own.

No! I would never bring my whittled down stub of a pencil to school. If only I had that beautiful tall new pencil that Daddy first handed me, I would be like the others. Well, almost. I still wouldn't match because my pencil was red. But Sarah said it's all right not to match. I wasn't like the rest of the class in other ways, too. I had already read all the yearly readers and was reading some advanced books from the library. I was better at math than anyone in the room, even James. Once I overheard Mrs. Goggins tell Mrs. Hopkins, "Maggie might as well skip grade school."

And I could outrun anyone, especially the boys; I always won at chin-ups; and I could hit a softball a mile, just like Daddy. But still, I didn't have my own pencil. It was okay. A little bit okay . . . and a whole lot embarrassing.

Right after lunch, James stood up and looked out the windows, "Gosh, look outside, it's black as night. It's a blizzard!"

I looked up just as I heard Mrs. Goggins say, "Maggie, hurry, get your coat and things. The bus children are going home. Now."

Outside it was as cold as it was dark.

"Mrs. Hopkins said your sisters will come for you, Maggie." Mrs. Goggins was just a few steps away, but her voice sounded distant in the wind. "Wait here inside the porch."

I shivered as two figures moved toward me in the darkness. The one running would be Celia, I thought; she's always in a hurry.

"Hey, this is fun, huh, Mag?" Celia yelled over the wind.

"I just want to get home," I yelled back. "I don't like blizzards," I said, stomping the ground with my foot.

"It may take a while. You both have to be patient," Sarah said, taking my dinner-bucket.

As we headed toward the headlights of the buses, icy sleet stung our faces. After we scrambled up inside, Elmer checked to see if all were present. He stood at the steps, his pale blue eyes were stern, and his blonde curly hair was covered in snow and sleet. "Looks like we're in for a blue norther," he said. "I'm going to try to get all of you to your homes before the storm gets worse." He winked at me. "You'll be better off at home than stuck here at school, don't you think?" Then suddenly solemn and serious, he turned to the others and ordered, "Sit still, no roughhousing, and you biggest boys be ready to jump out and push. I need each and every one of you to help me."

The steady sleet pinged on the windows and tapped a warning on the metal roof. As the bus began to move, I watched Elmer hook a chain of small metal dog tags around the back of the large rearview mirror. When he looked up to check on all of us, I caught his gaze. He smiled. We were off.

I loved Elmer, not as much as I loved Daddy, but almost. He was handsome and tall too, but younger. When he returned home from the war, he was touted as the town's decorated hero. He got his real job at the Farmers and Merchants' Bank and drove the school bus part-time. The kids behaved on his bus, whispering rumors of his bravery they'd heard from their parents. The boys especially bragged about riding the "Hero Bus." But Elmer always had a special smile for me. One time Sarah noticed and whispered, "You and Elmer sort of look alike. You could be his girl. You both have curly yellow hair and big blue eyes and you are both skinny." I giggled.

The bus churned through the deep snow. When we stopped, I could hear calls of "goodbye" as classmates stepped into the swirling dark. We watched each of them disappear down snow-covered lanes they knew by heart. "What if the storm makes them lose their way?" I said.

"Shhh, Elmer knows best," Sarah answered.

At every stop Elmer braked, waited, and honked the horn at long intervals, until he felt certain the children had found their house, or someone had found them.

When we left the gravel-topped roads, the drifts and swirling snow and sleet became worse. The bus moved inch by inch along the slippery ice. Time and again, the oldest boys jumped out and tried to push the sliding bus back toward the center of the winding lanes. We were creeping along through low-hanging tree limbs covered with ice. After many long dark miles, just a handful of us were left, huddled close together near the front of the bus. We held hands and kicked our feet because Sarah told us, "If we keep our circulation moving, we'll be warmer." Glancing up at the mirror, I saw Elmer's face, his forehead wrinkled with worry.

"I'm scared, Sarah. Are we near the Harrises' bridge yet?" I whispered.

"It's taking a lot longer, but we must be getting near," Sarah said. "I really can't tell where we are." She took my mittened hand. "Don't be afraid."

"But I am. I'm scared of that bridge even when it's sunny," I said as the bus slid to a stop. Elmer opened the door and motioned for the two Rahe boys to follow him.

The wind came whipping through the open door, bits of ice blowing up the bus steps onto Elmer's seat.

Sarah asked, "Did James help you with your boots and leggings?"

"Not today," I said. "I'll bet he's been at home for hours playing with his collie, Daisy." James lived across the street from school. He was lucky to live in town. Well, I thought, I guess I'm lucky too. "I'm lucky you made me these woolly leggings," I smiled. "They're hard to get on and off, but they're keeping me warm even today!"

Sarah laughed as Celia teased, "I wish I had some leggings! But, freezing or not, leggings or not, I'm not a fraidy-cat like you, Maggie. I am not scared of an old bridge."

I sat up taller, trying to toughen up like Daddy tells me to when I'm afraid. "Doesn't that creaky old bridge scare you, Sarah?"

Just then Elmer's voice called from the doorway. "All right now," he said. "We're going to walk to the Harrises' place. The wood bridge is too icy to chance it with the bus. Get your belongings and line up outside with a walking partner."

Elmer shut off the engine and cut the headlights. Closing the bus door, he hurried to us with a long rope. I watched as he tied all of us together in pairs, one on each side of the rope, the way you would harness a team of horses. The ice hitting the abandoned metal bus sounded almost as loud as fireworks popping. Elmer took the lead, placing the boys at the rear of the group. My mittened hand touched Sarah's while Celia lined up in front of us with her best friend, Nadeen Harris.

Icy sleet stung our faces as we moved slowly, trying to find our footing with each new step toward the narrow, creaky board bridge.

Sarah leaned toward me. "When we walk across the boards, do not look down at the creek, and hold onto the rope with both hands."

Before stepping onto the bridge, Elmer called back, "Pretend you're marching. Take each step together."

We moved ahead, left foot, right foot, over and over, crunching a cadence over the ice-covered boards, inching forward, almost as one.

The sleet turned into huge snowflakes covering the rope, our gloves and coats. It was impossible to see a thing. I decided to hold my breath while we were crossing the slick boards. I always held my breath whenever I was afraid. Just when I was about to run out of air, Sarah announced, "We did it. We're on solid ground!" My good-luck breath-holding trick had worked again.

We surrounded Elmer, all talking at once. I thought I saw the almost-invisible row of tall cedars at the top of the steep hill. I pointed up and Sarah answered, "Yes. It's the Harrises' lane. We're nearly to our corner."

"Will we walk on home, Sarah?"

"We'll see what happens after we rest."

It was slippery going uphill. We held on to each other, grabbing the low bushes beside the road to keep from falling. Elmer helped us climb higher. Near the hilltop, I heard a loud whistle. Behind the whistle, a dog barked over another noise I suddenly recognized. "It's Daddy and Teddy with the wagon. It's Joe and Slim."

We called as loud as we could from the windy hill-top, "We're up here, Daddy!"

From below appeared a lantern-lit commotion. Teddy, running ahead, was urging the mules on up the hill. Daddy's whistles and clicking noises were creating a language that both dog and mules understood.

When Daddy called, "Whoa," the mules came to an immediate stop. "Good old Joe and Slim," I said, as Celia and I ran toward them. Their breath filled the crisp air with steam. "Look how proud they are."

The icy wind and snow whipped all around us as we crowded beside the wagon. Even Elmer was looking worried. He called to Daddy that he and the rest of the children would stay put at the Harrises' place for the night.

"Good idea," Daddy yelled over the wind, "you'll have no luck calling their families, though. Too much ice on the telephone wires. Lines are sagging and the phones are most likely dead already."

"We better go while there's still oil in the lantern." Daddy shook Elmer's hand, adding, "I don't know how you did it, Elmer. Fine job. We were sure worried about our girls. Haven't seen a storm like this in years."

Just then we heard Mr. Harris calling as he ran

down the lane toward us swinging his lantern. When he spotted his girls, Ruby and Nadeen, he pulled them to him, his voice catching in a sign of relief.

"Elmer, you and the kids better stay with us. It'll be more than one night, I reckon. It's a real blue norther," he shouted. "A miracle you made it this far. You're a brave one, for sure."

Once Joe and Slim circled back in the direction they'd come from, we pushed Teddy into the wagon next to us. He was ice-covered, his hair matted in clumps. He licked our mittens and shoes, turning circles in the hay before finding his own special spot for the ride home. His big eyes searched from one of us to the other, making sure we were each okay.

As we moved downhill, I turned to get a last glimpse of Elmer and the others. The Harrises led the Rahe boys, the Wilson sisters, the Tucker boy, and Elmer toward the snug farmhouse. In their flickering lantern light, I thought I saw someone waving to us. We'd been brave—but I was sure glad we were headed home.

We crawled under wool blankets and settled into the loose hay with Teddy's warm, wet body in the middle of the three of us. Daddy's clicking noises—his conversation with Joe and Slim—and the jingling harnesses joined the sound of the squeaking wagon wheels as they churned through the icy deep. The snow-laden trees hovered above us as we made our way past the four corners and through drifts that were already chest high on Joe and Slim. They strained, pulling, ever minding Daddy's mule talk. With a blanket, we made a tent over our heads against the pounding sleet, and I began to feel warmer. Safer. Daddy sat tall on the wagon seat, his woolly old overcoat and hunting cap with ear flaps blowing in the icy wind, the only protection he had from the weather.

Just as we came up the hill, the wagon began slipping sideways. We slid into each other and Teddy jolted upright—ready to jump. Sarah gripped him as Celia and I banged into each other. We had knocked heads, but we knew to hang on and stay calm. Daddy stopped the wagon, climbed down, and carefully edged his way up to Joe and Slim. He seemed to be whispering to them. We watched, crouching.

"He's speaking their language," Sarah said. "I swear, he can do anything when he decides to."

Slowly, the mules seemed comforted and coaxed by Daddy's whispers. Finding their rhythm, Joe and Slim began straining, pulling the wagon up the slick hill again. Daddy climbed up and settled back on his seat. I was glad when we seemed to be moving a bit faster, but just then, the wagon slipped sideways again, tipping violently toward a dark crevice, the deep ditch at the side of the narrow road.

Suddenly, we were sliding! "Hold on to me," Sarah cried, reaching out to me while Teddy began barking wildly. Just before the wagon landed in the ditch, I felt the wheels catch hold. From his topsy-turvy seat, Daddy quietly commanded, "Don't move. Even an inch. And Sarah, calm that dog. He'll spook the mules."

Once again, Daddy was on the ground, carrying the lantern high, inspecting the situation. "The wheels are frozen up. That's why we skidded. Celia, my axe is under the seat. Now, go slow, no shaking the wagon, and hand me the axe. I'll chip the wheels free of ice and we'll get moving. Don't worry, and Maggie, don't you be crying. Toughen up!"

He worked quickly, circling the wagon before crouching beside each wheel, hacking off big chunks of ice with the axe. This gave the mules a bit of rest, so that when Daddy once again held the lantern up near their heads, speaking his magic words and patting their necks, they barely moved about in their traces, they just kept blowing shuddering breaths into the cold air.

Then all of a sudden, Daddy began singing his favorite hymn, "In the Sweet By and By." And as we watched in amazement, Joe and Slim slowly began moving their heads up and down in time with his voice. It was as if they knew he was singing to them.

"He must have sung to them, plowing in the fields, when they were young," Sarah whispered.

"It looks as if they are remembering," added Celia, "I never saw such a sight."

"You know what?" I said, smiling, "I'd been wishing Daddy would find his old self today, and I think he just did."

Once again Daddy urged the mules slowly forward and this time the wheels caught. The wagon righted itself with a bang. We fell into the hay and sang along, our soprano voices high above Daddy's deep bass. We were moving along at a fast clip when we saw Daddy seize the moving wagon with one hand, swing himself onto the seat, then grab the reins. Laughing loud like a boy, he yelled, "Never a doubt."

"Well, I never," Sarah said. "Can you believe him?"

"I can," I said.

The mules began pulling faster. Celia laughed. "They know the way now. I bet they are thinking about hay . . . and getting out of this ice."

I stood and saw the dark outline of the cedar grove and rising streams of chimney smoke and yelled, "We're almost home!"

The yellow light in the kitchen windows beamed out onto the bare white hilltop. I saw Mama waiting for Joe and Slim to pull beside the front porch so we could tumble out of the wagon into her arms.

Celia and Teddy hurried to the barn with Daddy to hay Joe and Slim and the bull, sure that Mama would have already milked the cows herself, storm or no storm.

Stepping through the kitchen door, I smelled potato soup and cornbread. "My favorite supper," I said as I hugged Mama close, smelling the starch in her apron along with the good odor of onion on her hands.

"We've had a frightening day," confessed Sarah.

I looked at her. "I never knew you were scared, too! So maybe I wasn't such a baby." We laughed and hugged.

The room glowed from Mama's precious Aladdin coal oil lamps, and the red-hot, sizzling cedar logs in the big iron woodstove.

"Oh Mama, I'm so glad to be home, and guess what? Best of all, Daddy found his old self tonight. He sang to Joe and Slim. We sang too, even in the sleet."

Mama smiled. "My yes, they always loved it when we sang while we worked the fields. It seemed to keep them from getting stubborn."

Soon we were all gathered around the big table, taking turns telling about the sliding bus, how Elmer took charge, how brave the boys were pushing the bus, how scared we were marching across the skinny icy bridge, and how excited we were to see Daddy, the mules, and Teddy.

I looked at Celia. "Where is Teddy?"

"On the back porch."

"Mama, please, couldn't Teddy come into the warm kitchen just this once? He helped so much today, please, just this once. He's earned it," I pleaded. I saw Sarah staring into her plate and Celia glancing nervously at Daddy. They knew I was pushing it. It was not allowed.

"He'll just lay by the stove. He's so good," I ventured bravely, looking at Daddy.

Daddy caught Mama's eye, then nodded a tentative okay. No one spoke.

Sarah opened the rear door, whispering to her dog, encouraging him to enter a room he'd never seen before. He hesitated, shaking and licking his lips. Inside, he stopped and looked around the room. He stared at Daddy and, as I watched in disbelief, he slowly turned and went back through the door to his gunnysack bed on the cold porch.

Somehow Teddy knew where he stood with Daddy. I thought I saw Daddy almost smile, glad that Teddy was smart enough to know his place. But when Daddy caught me watching him, his blue eyes narrowed. I looked away.

After the dishes, Mama brought in a galvanized bucket, full of clean snow she had stashed in the icy pantry. I ran to get the milk pitcher and Watkin's Vanilla flavoring. Sarah brought the sugar canister, a large cream-ware bowl and spoons. The bucket emptied fast as we stirred a batch of creamy colored, sweet smelling snow ice cream.

"For such brave girls," Mama toasted. Celia said, "And Joe and Slim—and Teddy." I glanced at Daddy and added, "Daddy, too."

He'd seemed sad and distant all supper, even after the exciting wagon ride and his beautiful singing. I took my bowl to my warming bench behind the woodstove, to sip tiny spoonfuls, savoring the satisfied feeling a big serving of special snow cream gave me, but I worried with every bite. Daddy was not himself. Times were hard, I knew that. I knew it and I was afraid.

I remembered what Sarah said last week, "Maybe the truck will break so Daddy can't go to town to drink away his worry at Boots's Blue Moon or Lewis's Beer Joint." Mama had overheard her. I'd listened as Mama begged Sarah and Celia to be more understanding of Daddy. Mama saw Sarah's disgust and Celia's anger. She'd put her hands on her hips and told them, "He's torn up over our farm debt, he regrets taking the loan, and he's afraid he'll fail us. He thinks it's a scandal if you owe someone money . . . he'd rather take a beating than to take help from anybody, especially from the government. He has a lot on his mind." Then she hugged them both.

Sometimes on long, dark nights Mama and Daddy

used to tell stories of when they were first married, working together in the fields, through the Great Depression days, when work and food were scarce, and no one had a nickel to their name.

Mama talked about the dust storms they'd lived through when Sarah was a baby, of watching huge red-black clouds of dust moving toward the house. The dirt piled up inside the house so high it was difficult to breathe. They kept wet rags over their faces and were lucky they had one milk cow and a few chickens.

"We hadn't had good crops since 1932, and we were down to the last of the canned goods I'd put up in the cellar. Mostly though, I remember the wind and the mules . . . walking behind them, breathing the dirt. Don't you, Arley? How we talked to the seeds and prayed for rain that wouldn't come." She smiled, "But we had one another."

"We moved rent farm to rent farm trying to make a go." Daddy shook his head, then bragged: "Your Mama was skinny and small, but she could outwork two hired hands." Mama would just lower her head, but I could see a little smile on her face when Daddy would say, "It's the Cherokee in her."

By the time I was born, they'd lived long years of lost dreams, but they'd always been "in it together." They'd had such high hopes that this farm would be the one where they would be able to get ahead, have some cash and see a future. While most row crops failed, Daddy was king of cotton in these parts. It was as if he were a magician, able to coax it as it grew, but even huge piles of cotton had not been enough to pay off the farm loan. Daddy had seemed up to the task in the beginning with everyone counting on him, but day after day of worry about the crop failures and the government debt beat him down. I could see him change. The twinkle in his eyes and easy laugh was gone. He turned sullen. Whiskey became his rescue and our downfall. It was pulling him away from us. Away from our dream of home.

I watched Daddy slump in his rocker as Mama reminded us, "The old times were even harder than now, but we made it, and we're better off than lots of people. We don't have any cash, but we can live off this land. We're not hungry like some folks."

She must have thought we needed cheering, for she added, "Maggie, remember when I took you to sign up for gas rationing coupons in town? We still have many coupons left since we hardly ever go anywhere."

She glanced at Daddy, adding, "I'm so afraid our old truck might break down, but, oh lordy, I do wish we could go visit Grandma Judy-Bob!"

She went on, "And anyway, even if I thought the truck would make it, the tires are shot and patched over and over." She glanced at us and winked. "I heard you girls say, 'They're slick as snot,'" she said, laughing.

Daddy stirred. "Some fella at the service station told me that someone has figured out how to use cotton to improve rubber tires. The war effort needs a lot of rubber tires for airplanes. He said cotton prices are going up this year."

Celia clapped her hands. "That's good news for us, since you're the best cotton farmer in the whole county, Daddy."

Daddy suddenly leaned toward Mama. "It was okay to get the gas stamps, but you shouldn't have gotten those canned food stamps. I won't eat any of it."

He boomed, "I don't want anyone thinking we need government help." His fist struck the arm of the chair.

I cringed at his sudden flare-up. Had he found a whiskey bottle in the barn earlier? That would explain his mood change. Poor Mama was taking the brunt of his anger. I thought the sweet canned peaches those food stamps bought were worth his angry words, but I would never say it aloud.

Whenever he got riled up like that over the government, Mama always worked her magic. She went to him and rubbed his back and gently reminded him, "Arley, you know President Roosevelt's ideas, like the food stamps and farm loans are to help everyone, even us, get through these years. We've got to make it until the war is over and times get better. You know we can."

He closed his eyes and shook his head, but she kept on, "We're going to work this year's crops. It's going to be a good year. This year we'll raise enough money to pay off our Farm Security loan, and then we'll talk the bank into helping us buy this land."

We watched as she knelt beside him taking his hand, "Arley, look at me, I have my heart set on owning this farm, and so do the girls. We're not moving again."

She was propping him up. His sad blue eyes showed how much he needed her encouragement. So did I. I felt like crying, seeing him so weak, floating on the edge of being gone. I pictured how wild he had been ruining my pencil, cutting the rocker arms, and singing like a lost soul. He was giving up, and Mama was desperately trying to stop him from slipping away from us.

THREE

THE KITCHEN GLOWED GOLDEN YELLOW and the burning wicks swaying inside the glass globes seemed to be waving goodnight. "Let's get in some more wood. We'll need to keep the fire burning all night," Daddy said, opening the door to the back porch.

Sarah jumped to help him, while Celia and I undressed. Mama took a lamp and disappeared up the enclosed stairwell to turn down the beds and bring our floral flannel night gowns, the soft quilts and blankets to warm beside the woodstove.

"Let's get up early and explore the snow," I said to Celia.

We held a blanket close to the stove until we smelled the wool scorching.

"Ready, Celia?" Nodding, Celia started up the steps as Mama wadded the hot blanket to her chest and followed. She always bundled each of us girls inside her own warm wrap before pulling a mountain of quilts over us all. Celia complained she never knew which way to lie, since she couldn't move an inch under all the heavy bedding. I was always last up the stairs because I still slept next to Mama and Daddy in the old hired hands' daybed. It was narrow and short, and I had gotten so tall that I had to sleep with my legs bent.

The kitchen water buckets would be frozen by morning so Mama placed a deep pan of water under the stove where Daddy wouldn't step in it when he got up to stoke the fire during the night. With the last blanket warmed, Mama blew out the kitchen lamp and Daddy carried me up into the dim lamp light at the top of the stairs. I laid my head on his shoulder to see if I could smell whiskey, but upstairs was heavy with the odor of burning cedar logs, Vicks salve, and Mama's Pond's face cream.

Maybe Daddy hadn't had any whiskey tonight, after all. Maybe he'd just been tired and upset.

After the upstairs lamp was out, I said my prayers and reached out into the moonlight for Mama's warm and reassuring hand. Two squeezes meant goodnight.

We'd been asleep for a long while when we heard it. A coyote! Then there were several howling from the slope by the creek. They were working their way toward the house. Toward us.

"Come and get us, Mama," Sarah's voice, hardly above a whisper, muffled from within her blanket cocoon came floating from their room.

The moonlight on the bright snow silhouetted the coyotes' every move. From the windows, we saw two animals move into the clearing between the henhouse, the barn and the house.

"Where did Daddy go?" I said.

"To get the shotgun," whispered Sarah.

"Man, they're bold, coming right up to the house," Celia said.

"They must be awfully hungry. I've never known them to come into the clearing before," added Mama.

Suddenly Celia gasped, "What about Teddy? He hasn't barked." A gun shot from below shook the window glass. The coyotes abruptly turned toward the creek.

In the moonlight, we watched as a third coyote raced into the clearing with something in his mouth. Running to catch his pack, he got caught in a deep drift. A second shot sounded from Daddy's gun. The coyote abandoned his catch.

"Lordy mercy, it's one of my hens!" exclaimed Mama. "That mean old devil got her."

The hen was a motionless lump on the snow. Daddy walked slowly into the clearing, gun in the crook of his arm, while Teddy suddenly appeared, racing after the coyotes. But he stopped abruptly, returning to make frantic circles around the hen. Daddy stared at the woods where the coyotes had disappeared. I thought, he looks so tall and brave, just like a hero must look. Then, with the injured hen in one big hand, he turned back toward the house.

We clambered down the frigid stairs, plucking sweaters and jackets from the hooks beside the wood-stove, then watched Mama checking the hen. Clucking and shaking nonstop, the hen was near impossible for Mama to hold at first, but despite everything, the hen's beady eyes stared straight at Mama. "I think she's listening to you, Mama," I said. "Look how she's moving her head from side to side."

Sarah bent over the hen, then gasped. "Her foot is gone! The coyote bit off one whole foot."

"Poor thing. We'll have to keep her inside for a while," Mama murmured. "She's been one of my best settin' hens. I guess she'll figure out how to get around on this stump. She was in my flock when we were first married and lived on the Morris place."

Mama took the hen to the pantry to look for a box and some rags. Suddenly, Daddy turned and looked toward Mama, "Tonight sure reminds me of a night at the Morris place. I thought of old Bulger when Teddy took off after the coyotes. You remember, Lou?"

I knew from the expression on Mama's face that she knew this story all too well.

"It was a lot like tonight," Daddy said. "There had been a big snow and the moon was nearing full. We had a bulldog then named Bulger. I guess I have never told about him before. He was mean-looking, squatty, well-built, a fighter, with teeth sticking out above his upper lip. I have to say, he was the only dog I ever liked much. He worked hard, just like another field hand and always had the cattle in line. He'd nip them on the leg if they didn't follow. He was a true watchdog and not afraid of anything. We set much by him. He was a prize. But on that night, Bulger took on more than even he could handle. He tangled with coyotes, fighting with a whole pack of them. He was as fast as the devil, though, and broke free in the chase. He woke us up barking for help. I shot at the coyotes right through the porch screen door and not a second too soon. Bulger ran into the yard and right up onto the porch. We let him come in the house, didn't we, Lou?"

Mama nodded, "He had never been inside before," she said, winking at me.

"What happened to Bulger, Daddy?" Celia asked.

For a minute, he hesitated, and then added, "We were cutting hay that following summer. Mr. Hawks, who helped us farm, was on the mower behind the mules, and Bulger, as smart as he was, must've been chasing something and didn't notice the mower. He was so damaged I had to put him down." He looked at Mama. "It almost killed us."

Back in bed, I was glad Teddy's bout with the coyotes tonight had reminded Daddy to tell about Bulger. Maybe Daddy would see Teddy in a new light. Losing Bulger—for Daddy—had meant something bigger than just losing an animal. I was happy he'd loved a dog that much. It explained why he was just "all right" with Teddy, but never touched him or spoke kindly to him. Maybe Daddy couldn't betray his loyalty to Bulger. Daddy and Bulger seemed a lot alike, kind of ornery but hardworking and brave, especially brave against coyotes.

I tossed and turned, picturing Daddy standing with his gun in the snow. I remembered a snapshot of him I'd seen in the leather picture box we kept in the summer parlor. Daddy was in a baseball uniform, smiling broadly and shaking hands with someone in the crowd around him.

He'd looked handsome and happy, but if he'd been so happy, why didn't he tell stories about his baseball days? He never talked about his past. He'd never even told us about Bulger before tonight.

For some strange reason, Mama hadn't talked about those years either, until we made her angry once driving home from Grandma Judy-Bob's. All the hints we'd ever heard of Daddy's baseball greatness usually spilled out at Grandma Judy-Bob Pate's house when Mama's whole family gathered. Everyone was there but Daddy. Mama just passed it off as, "My folks don't get along with him, so he doesn't go, and I don't ask them to our house."

That time, before the truck and tires got too dangerous to go the long miles to Grandma Judy's house, we'd heard Grandma remembering how much fun they'd had in the beautiful ballpark, filled with people from all over the county, just to see Daddy play ball. "So many kids hung around him, they nicknamed him Doak, and grown folks in the bleachers called him Tarzan. When he came to bat, everyone always yelled, 'Never a doubt!'"

"Everyone was a little baseball crazy and really crazy for your good-looking Dad. He was so strong. It seemed like he had a little magic," Grandma boasted. "I think your Great-Grandma Caroline would have claimed him for her own." Everyone had laughed, but I wasn't sure what was so funny, except that Grandma Caroline Pate was Indian and Daddy was not one bit Indian.

Uncle Gordon had added, "Arley was the best player in the Oklahoma minor leagues, for certain. He was the strongest man I ever witnessed. Most folks agreed on that. Those days, Arley had it all."

*
**

When we drove home from Grandma's, I asked, "If Daddy was so great, then why did he give up baseball?"

"No one ever mentions that," Celia added. "Why won't you tell us the reason he quit ball?"

We'd pushed her, and even though Mama was frustrated with us, she pulled the truck to the roadside and sat facing us, finding her words as darkness fell.

"He was amazing, girls," she said, "Like Grandma said, everybody *was* crazy over him."

"His good luck with baseball and our strong love gave him direction and purpose. But his family was troublesome. As Daddy became popular, his younger brother had difficulty accepting Daddy's success. He was constantly in trouble with the law and always drinking whiskey."

"One summer night, Bill caused a ruckus during the ballgame. He was not himself, and after the game, Daddy decided he'd better take Bill home to his family. On the road in Bill's truck, they got in a scuffle that somehow caused Daddy to lose control. When the truck overturned, Bill was killed and Daddy, well, Daddy did not have a scratch on him."

I caught Mama's hand. We sat without speaking in the dark truck. Mama, quiet a long while, finally added, "Arley was so badly affected, he simply shut down. He stopped playing ball. He turned away all offers of help and listened to no one. Not his coach, not his closest friend, Tom. Not even me. He blamed himself for Bill's lost life. Farming gave him an escape from baseball's glow. Farming came harder for him, but it was his own world, and he could plow his pain under, furrow after furrow."

Sighing, she said, "He gave up baseball, and hid at the farm. He felt like he didn't deserve all the good things he had. Even the newspapers wrote that no one could believe he gave up what surely would have been an amazing career."

"Bill and Daddy had the same smile and kind of charm. But Bill lured Arley into whiskey time and again." She looked away, as if it hurt to remember. "Before the accident," she continued, "I swear Arley worried more about Bill's problems than he did ours. He was convinced he needed to take care of Bill and his family. His wife, Kate, and their kids were often hungry and sickly. One chilly fall evening we went to help Kate with Bill, who'd been in trouble. Kate and I watched them foolishly passing a whiskey bottle back and forth. We sat near the open fire she kept burning in a small rock-lined bed just outside the kitchen door. She always had a coffee pot boiling on the edge and sometimes she'd fry onions and potatoes in an iron skillet over the flames. She kept a pile of firewood nearby."

"I remember this plain as day," she added. "About dusk a giant man showed up, yelling and cursing Bill, demanding money. By that time Bill was falling-down drunk, and Arley was not much better. Daddy stepped into the argument taking Bill's side of the fight—and the blows. Words and fists flew. As they circled one another, the huge man, touting and teasing Arley while cursing Bill, suddenly pulled a switchblade. I saw the blade shine in the firelight, then he lashed out cutting Arley's hands and arms. When I saw the blood spurt, I moved closer to the woodpile. I picked a solid log, moved behind the cutter, and struck him from the rear. He fell, landing in the fire. Arley dragged him from the flames and rolled him onto his back. Then he shook his head, grinned, and handed me the knife. 'It must be the Cherokee in you!'

"See, girls, Daddy was Bill's protector and defender, but after the truck accident, instead of saving him, he felt as if he'd killed him. When the pain of that memory gets bad, he fills the dark hole with whiskey."

Swallowing hard, Mama looked straight at us, "He quit trying at almost everything. But he's kept my heart in spite of it all."

Huddled together on the narrow seat, we sat in silence. Each alone in our own thoughts all the way home on that dark, lonely night.

*
**

After the coyote scare, I still couldn't sleep. I kept remembering the story Mama had told of Daddy and Bill. Turning over, I peered up from my pillow to see Mama and Daddy asleep in the early daylight. The cold wind whistled around the windows, screeching in the screens. Tomorrow, I vowed, I would find that black-and-white photograph of Daddy in his baseball clothes. I wanted to see him when he was happy.

FOUR

WEEKS AFTER THE ICE STORM, our life seemed normal again. We'd resumed our morning trips to the bus with Teddy and Daddy. Most every morning, Elmer and Daddy had a friendly exchange as we climbed aboard; I was thrilled to see Elmer as a friend for us and for Daddy, too. Daddy hadn't acted crazy a single time since that terrible night with my red pencil.

But I'd started having bad daydreams and sometimes I'd have the same dream, even at school, even when the sun was shining. It was always the same. I'd be roaming and searching for Mama or Daddy, but I couldn't find them. I couldn't even find our house. I'd be listening for a familiar sound, but the only sound I could hear was the swooshing of the wind in the cedars. I could always find the windmill and I'd climb it, straining for any sound of an engine across the empty horizon. But there was nothing. Nothing, just me and the relentless wind. Lost. Alone. I kept these bad dreams to myself.

Daddy seemed better, distracted, but almost cheerful some days. We'd all gotten involved with the daily war reports on the radio. This Saturday morning, we'd heard about how Hitler might make a final stand in a place called the Bavarian Alps. And we learned that President Roosevelt was on a long journey overseas to an important meeting at Yalta, over in Russia.

Day after day Sarah told us the things she was learning in her history class. "Mrs. Loper says President Roosevelt has a silver tongue that inspires people. Every day she writes his quote 'We must. We can. We will.' on the blackboard."

I loved President Roosevelt. Grandpa Poynter had given me an FDR political pin he'd gotten when Mr. Roosevelt was running for office. I kept it in my cigar box with my secret keepsakes: a royal blue feather, a tig-ereye marble from James, a stack of Fleers bubblegum comics from Grandma Judy-Bob's house, my short red pencil, and the photograph of Daddy in his baseball uniform. I'd found it and swiped it from the leather box in the parlor.

I had heard Mama brag a million times about how Roosevelt had led this country during the Great Depression, through the challenges of the Dust Bowl and now in this war. He'd served longer than any other United States president, she was quick to say. She sure had a lot of faith in him.

Sarah and Mama really liked the President's wife, Eleanor, too. She traveled by train across the country meeting folks just like us. On her radio broadcasts called *My Day*, she said she was the President's eyes and ears. She told of the hard times she saw across America. She said that FDR's new programs plus the war effort could bring an end to the long Depression because people had work again. "All over the nation, men and even women are working in factories, building airplanes, sewing uniforms, and pulling together after so many heartbreaking years."

That sure *sounded* good, but in our Oklahoma countryside, there were few jobs and no factories. I worried about Daddy's fear of relying on government programs. How could families like ours survive without a little bit of help? I'd overheard Mr. Harris lecture Daddy. "Arley, you may be too scared to owe the government money, but you're at rock bottom; the Dust Bowl and Depression have nearly wiped us all out. We farmers need help, and we should take it. After all, we're helping the country, too."

I was wishing Daddy would listen to Mr. Harris when I heard Sarah click off the radio and call "Breakfast!" Then she announced, "Something big is about to happen now. FDR is going to meet Russia's Stalin and England's Churchill. Mrs. Loper said they aren't called the Big Three for nothing."

The war was all anyone talked about, I thought to myself. No one could forget when the Japanese bombed Pearl Harbor, and now four years later, everyone was *still* talking about war. I hoped it would end soon.

"I'd like some molasses," I sighed.

Mama pushed the molasses pitcher, a plate of hot buttermilk biscuits, and the butter dish across the checkered oilcloth. "Well, it's Saturday—churning day, Maggie," she said.

I made a face at Celia who was giggling at the prospect of my only real chore. I didn't like churning one bit—and it was every Saturday morning. It took so long. Only hair shampooing, with my tangled, curly hair, was even worse. I would rather be reading a book.

"Celia's job this morning will be to go into town with Daddy, then when the rest of us get our chores done, we'll ride into town with Mr. Harris." She nodded to Celia. "Celia, look for us."

I watched Daddy and Celia stack Mama's eggs and milk cans into our neighbor's rattletrap truck to deliver to the creamery in town, then climb in themselves. Mr.

Johnson's old Ford was as broken down as ours, but his tires had more tread and at least the engine was running smooth, hitting on all cylinders. After Daddy and Celia climbed in, I watched Teddy run after them to the main road. Then he suddenly stopped short, as if to wait for their return.

Washing the dishes, Sarah whispered, "Mama doesn't trust Mr. Johnson as far as she can throw him. Mama sent Celia to keep Daddy from spending the egg and milk money on whiskey."

I knew Mama suspected Mr. Johnson was a bootlegger, keeping his whiskey hidden along the deep creek that bordered our farmland. Once, she had said in disgust, "His whole crowd is lazy. Sneaky." It was an alarming thought, since Mama never spoke ill of anyone, that is, anyone except Lewis Mize and his saloon or Boots's Blue Moon beer joint. Well, sometimes she spoke poorly of Grandma Poynter, too. She wasn't a bootlegger, but Mama didn't approve of the fact that she'd encouraged her sons to drink whiskey when they were young!

I walked into the pantry determined to face my churning job squarely. It wouldn't be so bad if I could churn by the big window beside the front porch, but I saw the churn was already nearly half full of heavy cream. I asked anyway.

"Well, that's fine. Let me show you a clever way to move a heavy churn," Mama said, pushing the wood dasher down as far as it would go. She handed me the lid and I placed it over the long wooden handle, sliding it down onto the rim. Then she took the dasher handle in one hand and, with the other, leaned the entire churn over at an angle and rolled it right through the door and across the kitchen.

I followed, grinning. Mama knew how to do everything.

I placed a stool beside the churn. Not being able to think of any other way to stall the job, I started plunging the dasher up and down. I knew the important thing was to keep a rhythm so the cream would form beads of butter. Even if it was boring, I knew exactly how to make butter and I loved eating it.

While I worked, I watched Sarah carry a box of scrap wallpaper, old ribbon, and trims to the table and begin to sort them into piles.

As I pushed the dasher handle up and down, I started singing, "Up and down, up and down, I hope we go to town."

Sarah laughed, "That's clever, Maggie. I'll bet we could make up a longer song. Want to try?"

Soon the noise of the dasher kerplunking inside the crockery churn had us laughing and putting words together in a flurry of sounds.

Sarah was the smartest girl in her class. She'd be fifteen near Valentine's Day. She and I had Daddy's pale blue eyes; she was rail thin with chestnut colored hair that she pin-curled almost every night. She devoured books and had perfect straight-A grades. In fact, Sarah taught me to love books. She sewed on the Singer foot treadle machine better than Mama, Aunt Polly, and Grandma Judy-Bob put together. I was always careful never to complain about my itchy wool leggings and coat because she made them for me during the scorching heat of last summer.

Lately, I'd heard her whispering to Celia that Daddy had stopped taking care of things at the barn. She pointed out how he seemed distracted, roaming the cow pastures and red dirt fields. Sarah watched him even closer than Mama, and whenever Sarah worried, I worried too.

Mama finally came inside after doing Celia's regular chore of filling one water bucket after another using the hand pump at the well and carrying them from the pump all the way to the back porch table. It was a huge chore to always keep the buckets full. "Whew," Mama said, "No wonder Celia was glad to trade her chore for a trip in an old rattletrap truck." She glanced at me and saw me smiling, "It's good to see you so happy, Maggie." She smiled, too.

"Listen, Mama," I announced. "We made up a song." Then Sarah and I sang out to the beat of the dasher as I pushed it up and down.

Mama hugged me. "My butter maker is also my song maker. I like that. I think you've finished both jobs."

"I'll check it," I said, climbing off the stool. But as I stood, I noticed a mysterious black car, nearing our lane.

I watched as a strange man hurried across the dry grass toward the front porch.

"Butter's done," I yelled behind me as I dashed out the front door, trying to head him off. Could he be that Farm Security man I'd heard Daddy talk about? The one who "tells about farming from behind a desk." What if he'd come to tell us we had to go? Where could we move?

When he saw me, the man stopped. I stopped too. We eyed each other. Then I moved toward him.

"Good day, little lady," he said tipping his tan felt hat. "You're going to catch a fine cold if you don't put on a coat."

I nodded, and then blurted out, "Do you sit at a desk where you work?"

He stared at me for a minute, then laughed, "No. I never could stand a desk. Sort of hems a fella in, I think. I'm a trader-man myself. I'm Mr. Wright and pleased to meet you."

"You must be here to see my mama." I led him toward the door. Teddy sniffed Mr. Wright's heels, inspecting him along the way.

My wide grin announced Mr. Wright to Mama. The country trader-men were usually funny and exciting. They were from the outside world and full of stories. Their style was to spin a little gossip, tell who traded what, and pass out a lot of flattery while allowing isolated farmwomen to shop at home.

Mr. Wright spread his trade wares on the table.

Mama had barely looked at everything laid out in front of her before she said, "I'll trade you one fat hen for a tin of Watkins black pepper."

"Nope," he said.

"How about two hens for a subscription to the *Kansas City Star* newspaper?" she asked, but he shook his head no again. Mama frowned. "We need the war news and the sewing patterns in the newspaper too."

Clearly the trader didn't want hens. He said, "Scrap metal, ma'am, I'm wanting scrap metal. It's needed for the war effort."

I interrupted proudly, "Sarah's class won the school scrap iron drive, Mr. Wright. Sarah took the most and got an award."

Mama said, "Well, I've got one used-up car battery and three iron plow points that might interest you, Mr. Wright."

"Sounds good. I'll offer you three pairs of nylon hose and the pepper.

Three pairs of nylon hose would've swayed most

women, but Mama had her eye on other things and thought it better to go barelegged than use up her chance for trading on stockings that would need darning sooner or later. She shook her head and would not budge.

Sarah had been eyeing *The Searchlight Cookbook*, opening the cover and fingering the pages, and because Mama noticed it, she said, "The newspaper, the pepper, and the cookbook and we have a deal, Mr. Wright."

I followed Mr. Wright to his dusty black sedan to watch him load his trade things in the trunk.

Looking around at me, he smiled, "Were you hoping someone who sits at a desk would come today?"

"I'm hoping he never comes. He's the Farm Security man from the government. He could make us move. I'm glad you're not him."

"Well, I'm glad too," he said. Then his hand reached out for mine. "Goodbye little lady, you still need a coat on. Yessir, you're sure going to have a cold."

I waved as he pulled out of the yard. He must not know how hard it is for country girls to catch a cold. After all, it was February, and the sun was shining.

※
※※

Later that afternoon, Mr. Harris, Ruby, and Nadeen drove into our lane, honking the horn on their red Chevrolet four-door deluxe. Mr. Harris had bought it brand-new from Macy's Chevrolet. "Cash on the barrelhead. I bought it for Daniel," he told anyone who would listen, "so it will be waiting for him when he returns." He was proud of his only boy, fighting in the war in Europe. But Mr. Harris was afraid to drive the car into town. Driving in traffic scared him to death. He always asked Daddy or Mama to take him on into town or even further—all the way to Oklahoma City if he needed.

In my freshly polished white high-top town shoes and good Sunday school dress, I skipped down from the porch, thrilled just to stand next to the shiny red fender, sucking in the smell of new rubber and cloth upholstery. Sarah and Ruby were busy combing their hair, "Just in case we see some town boys," Ruby said. I thought she was boy crazy. I'd watched her tease and flirt on the bus. Flirting looked disgusting to me.

Nadeen and Celia jumped into the back seat, pushing to the far side. Nadeen, Celia's best buddy, teased me mercilessly—about being the baby, about James from school, about almost everything! I let her get away with it on account of Nadeen being "nervous" and not having a mama at all at their house.

They were, for certain, our best neighbors. Mr. Harris was a lot older than Daddy, but he always tried to help him. He raised the finest black diamond watermelons in the county, but he took no credit, just said it was the sandy soil. Mama said he was a modest man who owned a lot of land and worked it well. I thought Mr. Harris was lonely. His faded blue eyes had a faraway look. He tried to cover his sadness with frequent little coughlike chuckles.

Now he sat in the wide front seat next to Mama, as she smoothly guided the wonderful smelling palace-on-wheels toward town. I squirmed, the car seat itching my legs. "Mohair," explained Nadeen.

The automobile was just another one of the many differences between the Harrises and us Poynters. Some people could just trust that everything would be all right. They had an air of certainty that prosperity seemed to shore up. But one thing the Harrises didn't have was a mama to drive a red car to town. Their mama lived in an asylum down in Oklahoma City, and no one ever said "nervous breakdown" out loud. The Harrises had their own kind of failure, and somehow it allowed them to understand others.

Anyway, maybe this trip to town in the beautiful car was hopeful. I daydreamed for a bit, pretending this was our car and we were coming from a farm that we really owned. But did Daddy really want to own a farm the way we girls and Mama did? He just couldn't give up on *this* dream like he had given up on baseball, could he? Maybe the Depression and the hard times of the Dust Bowl when there was no work or money, when Okies like Daddy had barely held on, had simply whipped him. Even I knew about the Okies who had left and gone to California hoping for work and a new start. At least Daddy had stayed on the land. He had stayed with Oklahoma.

Maybe now it would be better. Mama promised there was a chance for security and so had Eleanor Roosevelt.

My hopefulness traveled all the way past the cemetery and onto the edge of town where Mama began worrying aloud, "I thought for sure we'd meet Mr. Johnson's truck with Celia and Daddy way before this."

Crescent was a small town of maybe four hundred people. Everyone knew everyone else's business. As we turned left onto Main Street and passed Jack's gas station near the train depot, I felt a twinge of pride riding into town in a fancy car instead of our own dilapidated truck.

Mama slowed down, then stopped at the intersection near the creamery. "Keep a lookout for Mr. Johnson's truck, girls."

As we drove along Main Street, Sarah was the first to spot Celia. She was sitting on the curb, slumped, in front of Lewis's saloon. Mr. Johnson's truck was parked next to her. The red Chevy suddenly filled with a hard, lonely quiet, a silent fear of what might come next as Mama turned into the parking space next to her.

Celia rushed to us, her crying red eyes wild. "I failed, mama. I could not stop him. I tried and tried," she said. Suddenly, I wished to be anywhere but here. I knew Daddy had slipped to the bad place again. I clutched on to Sarah as Mama left us, slamming the car door behind her. Her town high heels made a sharp clicking noise as she stepped up onto the curb.

Main Street was still busy with shoppers this sunny afternoon. Mostly, it was farm people like us, trading eggs, getting a few groceries, and if they were lucky enough to have some extra money, going to the movie show next to the Farmers & Merchants' Bank where Elmer worked. But the real show was about to begin right here at Lewis's place as Mama walked straight as a soldier toward the door. I knew most women never darkened a bar room door, but Mama was no ordinary woman.

I always thought Mama was beautiful, but just now she was beautiful in a new way. Like Mr. Harris's shiny red car itself, she was powerful and conspicuous.

Mr. Harris lagged behind Mama, slapping his pant legs and shifting his hat nervously, following her as fast as he could into the bar.

Yelling and the sound of breaking glass from inside suddenly broke the silence. Loud voices came swelling out onto the sidewalk. Celia covered her ears and began to sob. As Sarah tried to calm her, she jerked away angrily. "He is not the Daddy I know. Why is he doing this? What will happen to us?"

Just then, Mama and Mr. Harris rushed out from the bar. Without a word, Mama hurriedly backed the car out of the parking space, drove down the street, abruptly turned the corner and then pulled into the alley behind the buildings. This created a stir of curiosity among the street onlookers, who'd pointed and followed.

If this hadn't been enough, there in the alley behind the rear bar door, Daddy and several men were struggling in a loud argument. As the car drew near, one big man in a blue work shirt reached out and struck a blow to Daddy's face. I watched in horror as blood spurted from his nose. Sarah, Celia, Nadeen, and Ruby screamed and covered their eyes. But I couldn't look away. The car jerked to a stop just as I saw Daddy draw his fists back and hit the blue-shirt man with what seemed like ten or more punches in the stomach right under his heart. Finally, Daddy threw his right fist hard under the other man's chin. Both men went down at the same moment, falling first to their knees before their faces hit the dirt.

I was scared, more scared than I had ever been, and shaking. But I was intrigued; those stories must be true about Daddy being the strongest man ever. I whispered, "Sarah, he is so strong, I can't believe my eyes. He's too strong, maybe."

Mama, Mr. Harris, and Mr. Johnson half-dragged, half-carried Daddy to the car, pushing him into the passenger seat. His shirtfront was covered with blood and his hair was full of dirt and grass, which fell onto the spotless mohair seat. I heard Mama say, "Johnson, you are a no-count neighbor, and I'll never trust you again."

Mr. Harris scooted under the steering wheel into the middle of the seat. Mama jumped behind the wheel and put the car in gear. As she pulled onto the street, Celia pounded the car seat with her fist. Even Celia could not pretend happiness today.

Sarah held me in her lap, squeezing my hands with such anger that it practically cut off my circulation. I smelled the whiskey, sharp, fierce and frightening, just like before when bad times set in. That hopeful daydream I'd had on the road to town was gone. No one spoke. The Harris girls stared at the houses on the edge of the town and then at the empty fields as we approached them like it was their one true mission in life. Mama turned corner upon corner along the deserted red road, finally pulling into our lane where Teddy still sat. Waiting.

At the farmhouse, Mama, Mr. Harris, and Sarah lifted Daddy out and dragged him, limp as a rag, through the rear screen porch and into the spare room off the kitchen where, as Mr. Harris said to Mama, Daddy could sleep it off.

Darkness surrounded the house, yet the big western sky glowed a fierce red orange as Mr. Harris drove off, leaving us wondering how we would cope.

The evening was chilly. As Sarah lit the lamps and built a fire, Mama hurriedly peeled potatoes and onions to fry for supper, reminding Sarah to stir the skillet often.

Then, she turned, reached for Celia, and walked to Sarah and me, as we stood beside the cookstove. Touching each of our faces for a moment, she told us, "We will not fail. We must love him no matter what. It will take that special Cherokee strength passed on to us from Great-Grandmother Caroline. We must stay strong together."

She hugged us. And then, as I watched, Mama and Celia carried the lantern through the darkness toward the barn, where Teddy had already moved the cows to be milked.

As the smell of fried potatoes filled the air, I huddled on my warming bench behind the big stove. I thought about being part Indian, about what having Indian strength must mean.

I wondered about this powerful Great-Grandmother who must have been about my age when she walked the

Trail of Tears all the way from the Carolinas to Fort Smith, Arkansas. Great-Grandmother Caroline survived to tell her story. Some incredible willpower must have guided her path, even as a young girl. I felt lonesome for a woman I never knew. I decided I would try to be like her—strong for Mama.

FIVE

THE ROOM WAS PITCH BLACK when I woke with a start. Teddy's constant barking signaled trouble. Mama was not in her bed, but the clean odor of Pond's Cold Cream still wrapped the room. I heard shouting, then a flurry of words. Something was wrong. I climbed out of my own bed onto Mama's, then felt my way through the dark to the top of the stairwell. The door at the bottom was ajar, and a pale light shone on the floor below as I crept down the steps.

I heard Daddy slinging loud and hurtful sounding words. Instead of singing, like the night he whittled my pencil, he was yelling dangerous and threatening words like, "Get out of here, I don't want your help." He was talking nonsense. I knew this was a much worse kind of drunken stupor. The noise he made falling down and crashing into the chairs was scaring Teddy, who was shut out on the porch and barking danger. It was scaring me too.

Pushing the door open wider, I saw Sarah and Celia crouched by the oak table. Daddy was by the cookstove, threatening Mama and trying to push her away from him.

Suddenly Sarah stood up. "Stop that right now." She took a step forward. "You don't scare me."

I saw Daddy freeze, his eyes wild.

I burst into the room.

Then Celia's angered voice rose. "Leave Mama alone and leave us alone too."

Suddenly, Daddy turned. He lurched toward the table and in a lightning-fast move, pitched a burning oil lamp over my sisters, hitting the wall behind them. The lamp splintered as flames engulfed the curtain. Sarah ran for me, but I pushed her away as I tried to get to the fire. Mama rushed to it, too, but Celia stood wordless. Helpless.

With the fire taking hold behind her, Mama's silhouette was frightening. Over the chaos, she ordered, "Girls, run now, run to your place in the cedars and stay."

Sarah and Celia sprang to life, running hand in hand, dragging me between them across the dry grass.

Scrambling and afraid, we ran toward my swing in the dark stand of cedars.

Here we squatted on the slope, catching our breath, fear enveloping us.

From the top of the ditch, we could see orange flames in the kitchen windows. I tried to breathe through my sobs. I was thrashing in the dirt and yelling over and over, "How can Mama fix this?"

Sarah pinned me flat against the side of the slope. "Stop it," she said, her voice full of authority. Then she pulled Celia over to me and, in the same commanding voice, ordered Celia, "This is your job. Do not leave this spot. Stay with Maggie until I come back for you. I mean it."

Celia and I watched in horror as Sarah ran right toward the fire, onto the porch and straight into what was surely hell.

Clinging to each other, we could hear Teddy barking above muffled voices, and the up-and-down squeak of the hand pump at the well and clanging metal. Suddenly out of nowhere, Teddy bounded into the cedar thicket and straight into our laps. The cold night breeze caused my rope swing to move slightly, like lost dreams rising out of Mama's kitchen, moving across the dry, yellow grass and into the dark ditch.

Later, huddled on Mama's smoke-filled bed, she told that when we'd run to the cedars, Daddy had passed out, falling to the floor, so that she'd dragged him out to the rear porch. There she'd snatched the ever-ready water buckets to quench the burning curtains and the floor fire. She then grabbed the unfinished quilt she'd been making to beat and gain on the leaping flames near the cookstove, where most of the coal oil had landed in the corner. Once inside, Sarah had freed Teddy from the porch so that he could find Celia and me. Then using uncommon speed, Sarah refilled the porch buckets at the water pump, running in and out faster than seemed humanly possible. Finally, they had overwhelmed the blaze.

When I saw them step off the porch, I whispered, "They're coming." Celia impulsively jumped and ran to join them, eager to be as grown-up as Sarah and a part of the saving of us.

I'd hung back, frozen to the dirt, hugging Teddy and shivering from both the cold night air and fear. Mama and Sarah could accomplish anything they set out to do. But how in the world could Mama fix Daddy?

Once Mama and Celia and Sarah were with me, we hugged each other, clinging to Mama's deep resolve.

Then with Teddy and my sisters leading the way, Mama gathered me close and followed them. The only sound was a night bird making its lonely ominous call.

**

Every day of February since that unforgettable Saturday had become a glum quiet. We moved listlessly through our chores, seldom chatting or laughing. The odor of smoke in the kitchen was a constant reminder of the fight and fire. A sad emptiness filled the dark evenings.

These mornings, Daddy stayed slumped in his chair. We even stopped saying "aw-re-vore" in the morning, when we left the house with Teddy.

The kids on the bus grew quiet when we climbed aboard, sometimes whispering as we passed down the aisle. One morning after Elmer greeted me, he reached up and patted my shoulder. In spite of our starched dresses, curled hair and pretty ribbons he seemed aware of the sadness in the three of us. A boy at the back of the bus stared at me and grinned. "Where's your dad this morning? He's probably loaded. Your dad's got a drinking streak as wide as the Cimarron River." I hurried into a bench seat and dropped my head, but Sarah sat proud and tall, and Celia offered a muffled, "Shut up."

Elmer must have overheard. He stopped the bus, grabbed the boy by the arm, dragged him off the bus, and whipped him, then stood by the embarrassed boy while he apologized to us.

Elmer turned to the other students and said, "No one is perfect, but on this bus, you will be pretty close to it. I'll not tolerate cruel and hurtful words."

I was mortified, but grateful for Elmer's support.

When we reached school, we hung back to thank him.

Elmer smiled and pointed to the dog tags dangling from the mirror.

"These belonged to a buddy of mine in the war. He was a mess . . . and I was too. Sometimes men lose their way, but they can find it again. We did. So these remind me to stay strong and not lose hope. Just remember that and keep your heads high."

*
**

That evening, Celia and I overheard Sarah tell Mama that someone in her class was talking at school about Daddy's fight behind Lewis's bar. Sarah said, "It embarrassed me to tears, but I didn't respond."

I was sure glad no one knew about the kitchen fire. Even the Harrises couldn't know. It had to remain our secret.

Sarah and Celia worked even harder to keep their top grades. Ignoring Daddy, they worked their chores, trying to avoid him whenever they could. More and more they were turning against Daddy.

So, there we were. Mama and I the only ones left praying that Daddy would come to his senses.

*
**

It was said that when I was born, Daddy was so disappointed I wasn't a boy that he was drunk for three days. Folks said Daddy was a hard worker and a good guy, but he could also be a real scoundrel. He had planned to name me Samson. Every now and then he calls me his little Samson. He thinks I take after him with my muscles and strong will. Truth is, I'm small built and wiry, but even Mama admits I have his uncommon strength. Whenever Celia calls me Samson, I never laugh. Because in my heart, I know I must be Samson-strong for him. I need to help him find his way again like Elmer said he could. I can't give up on him . . . he needs me. But day after day, I feel his sorrow and see him retreat. I was sad he'd stopped walking with us to the bus in the mornings. I knew Mama's heart was set on keeping this farm. How would we go on if we lost it?

On the Saturdays following the fight and the fire, no one went to town, especially not Daddy. Mama painted over the black burn marks at the window and in the corner. She even painted the scorched linoleum. I suspected that while we were at school, Mama worked her magic spirit on Daddy. I could almost hear her encouraging words, and I thought I could sometimes see a little bit of blue sky around him.

Daddy kept busy at the barn, preparing for the huge task of spring planting. He and the mules, Joe and Slim, plowed the garden, turning over the soil first in big rolls and then smoothing it out with a harrow before preparing the planting rows. We always planted potatoes near Valentine's Day, even if it snowed. Most planting was ruled by the Farmers' Almanac and the phases of the moon. At least this was something—a plan—we could depend on.

***

Soon it would be Valentine's Day. For as long as I could remember, we always celebrated the same way. For days we chose scraps of leftover wallpaper, fabric, and ribbons and secretly created cards for one another. This year, as usual, on the night before, Mama set the breakfast table and turned the plates upside down. She said it was an old Dust Bowl trick to keep the dust from the plates. Before bed we would slip our homemade valentines under the plate where each family member always sat. At breakfast, when everyone turned their plate right-side-up, we would share our creations. Homework and valentine-making had carried us through the long nights after the fire. I'd chosen a scrap of the floral parlor wallpaper, and some white eyelet lace, then trimmed my cards with bright red rickrack.

Despite Mama's calmness, her deep sighs worried me. I was beginning to see that Daddy drank whiskey because he was struggling. Maybe when he drank, he felt brave again. Sarah said whiskey gave him a false courage. I studied him closely and hoped maybe my card might make him smile. I printed on his valentine:

> Daddy and me,
> We're tough as can be.
> I hope he can see
> All he means to me.

SIX

THE WARM APRIL SUNLIGHT FELL through the kitchen window, shining on the corner by the stove, highlighting the new paint, black streaks, and scarred reminders of that awful night. Mama and Celia were draped over the table, tying knots of yarn to finish off a new quilt top. The radio faded in and out in the background.

Sarah sat stitching a jacket she would enter in the state 4-H club competition. She was listening closely.

I'd lined up my Betty Grable paper dolls in a row under the buffet. I was curled under there too, hearing the drumbeats and the solemn voices from the radio above me. President Roosevelt had died. I wanted to cry; it was so sad.

Sarah said, "I'll bet the whole nation is listening."

A favorite radio announcer, Arthur Godfrey, described FDR's last trip down Pennsylvania Avenue: the somber music, the marching soldiers, the horses drawing the funeral caisson, past the grand buildings in Washington D.C. I wondered if I would ever visit such an important place.

Since the fire, Daddy and Mama seemed to have made peace with one another. Not so with Sarah and Celia, though. There was a wall of silence between them whenever Daddy was present, despite his efforts to appear positive about the coming crop season.

Now a concern loomed over the uncertainty of how the new president might change things. *Things* being the Farm Security Act. It had been FDR's plan to help small farmers like us so we could keep the country supplied with cotton and wheat. The effort gave loans to farmers like us who couldn't get credit anywhere else, loans for equipment and seed. Although Daddy thought buying on credit was a yoke around his neck, he had succumbed.

Over the noise of the funeral, Daddy told us, "I think President Truman will end the Farm Security project, but he's going to let us farmers have until the end of the growing season to pay our debt. If we can pay off our loan this fall, like your Mama says, we might just prove ourselves to the bank and be able to buy the farm." He was trying, I thought, to win back Sarah and Celia's trust.

He had another surprise. "I am taking a job. Mr. Johnson and I were hired on the night shift to work on an oil drilling rig not far from here. I'll farm during the day." I glanced at Mama. I knew we desperately needed money, otherwise Mama would never have agreed to Daddy working as a roughneck on an oil well with the likes of Mr. Johnson. The night job was a good sign, though. Daddy was trying.

We had barely made it into spring, but Daddy had stayed sober all the way through the busy March planting season. He had been on the tractor every day sowing seeds in field after field. Now it was time to buy new baby chickens, plus we needed money to fix the truck and Mama feared the propane for the cookstove would be used up soon. Her tight-fisted savings were all but spent.

Day after day, Mama urged us forward, "See, if we keep our spirits up and if nature helps with money crops and the new calves, we'll own this place. Remember, President Roosevelt said it best, 'We must, we can, we will.'"

The summer and fall would decide it. At last, we had a plan. There was hope.

At the news of Daddy's new job, Celia hesitantly volunteered, "I can plow and help with all the chores, even the milking. I know I can."

"Thanks, Celia, I was hoping you would, and Grandpa Poynter is coming to help out, too," Daddy said. This third piece of good news made everyone happy. Grandpa Poynter was fun to have around. He was a good-humored man. I loved how he would play a trick on me, waiting for me to stand straight-legged with my back turned. He would gently knock me in the back of one knee. I would drop down and giggle and soon the two of us would be giggling so that we couldn't stop. I loved being in cahoots with him. Grandpa would be a tremendous help and a treat. And every night after supper he'd call me by the nickname he'd given me. "Hopadeedee," he'd say, "come light my pipe." I would, and the kitchen would be full of the smell of his Prince Albert tobacco.

*
**

I'd quit listening to the funeral long before I spied the arrival of Mr. Johnson's rattletrap truck. Not far behind I saw Mr. Harris on his big black horse, Midnight, riding down the lane. I thought it was curious that both men arrived at the same moment.

"It has gotten windy. I'll go fix the windmill to pump," I said to no one in particular.

I watched Teddy and Daddy greet the men near the barn. Why were they here? As the strong, gusty wind whipped my wool headscarf and thin cotton dress in all directions, I spotted the one-footed hen the coyotes nearly got last winter, wobbling under the lilac bushes. I picked her up. She had been so fussed over, she was quite tame now, although Mama's hens were all sort of tame. Mama always talked and sang to them as she fed them. Usually, she sang "My Blue Heaven," one of her favorite songs.

Once I had asked Mama. "Why do you sing? Do animals think? Do they have feelings?"

Mama had answered, "When I was young and asked Great-Grandma Caroline the same questions, she said the great spirit connects all living creatures, that all animals deserve gentleness and serve a purpose. Just between us, I think the hens lay more eggs if I talk and sing around them."

I put the hen in a nest close to the floor of the hen-house, patted her and headed toward the windmill.

First, I unlatched the pump handle and fastened the iron rod from the wheel onto the pump shaft. Then, I raised the wooden lever that released the taut wire holding the wheel in place. The tall iron skeleton roared into action. The big wheel pivoted to take advantage of the strong wind from the north. It gave out a terrible squeak. The up and down motion of the shaft began, and cold water poured from the pump mouth in measured, even bursts. I tugged the heavy pipe and hooked it over the pump mouth. The water flowed through the pipe toward the barnyard and into the cattle water trough. Each moving sound blended with the wind in a kind of song.

Then I tight-walked on the water pipe all the way to the water trough in the barnyard, balancing like a circus performer, step over step, before jumping to the ground.

Inside the barn was quiet. I saw that most of the winter hay was gone, but there was plenty left to jump on from the long rope swing. While I swung, the new kittens jumped about, hiding and playing in the hay bales.

Sunlight filtered in here and there, rays shining into the barn, the tiny dust particles bumping in every direction.

Wind whistled through the loft doors, muffling voices from the other side of the barn. The men must be near Old Hitler's pen, I thought.

I followed the voices, anxious to hear what they were saying. By climbing the wall ladder to the loft maybe I could eavesdrop. I scrambled up for a better view.

"Maggie, come quick! Watch it get its legs," Daddy called.

It was the first spring calf! "I'm coming!" I yelled.

It was an amazing sight to see a newborn calf try to stand up on all fours for the first time. Shaky and unsure, the calf kept falling, yet soon enough it found its legs. The white-faced calf had red, curly damp hair and beautiful sky-blue eyes, with the longest eyelashes, and a pink nose. As the mother cow licked the tottering newborn, the calf seemed to gaze directly at me. I glanced about and saw Old Hitler out in the far corner of his pen, horns and head lowered, his fearsome yellow eyes staring at the struggling calf, the men, Teddy and me.

When I looked back, Daddy was looking right at me. "Since it's almost your birthday, Maggie, maybe this calf should be yours."

The men chuckled as my face, puzzled at first, turned to disbelief. How could Daddy give up a valuable animal? I knew he would need to sell nearly every cow and spring calf next fall to help pay off the loan. How could he do without this one?

But Daddy must have realized that I never had an animal of my own. After all, Teddy had been Sarah's dog since she was a little girl. The mules belonged to Daddy, and Celia liked the Harrises' beautiful horses best. The chickens were Mama's, and the barn cats were too wild and fickle to belong to anyone.

I couldn't wait to tell my school friend James, and Celia and Sarah, and of course, Elmer! He'd be happy for me, too.

Dizzy with the prospect of my very own pet, I plopped beside the newborn calf, rubbing the moist hair on its slender nose as its pink, rough tongue, like sand-paper, tasted my fingers. I looked up, "Oh, Daddy, you mean it?" From the glint in Daddy's blue eyes, I knew he had given me something to hold onto. I smiled. "A birthday present. I'll call her April."

SEVEN

I LET THE SCREEN DOOR slam behind me. I was skipping
and running, singing along as the Mills Brothers' voices
blared from the Truetone through the open kitchen
windows.

Today everyone was happy, mostly because of
Sarah's success at school and a pending trip to town.
The purple lilac and white plum bushes blooming everywhere added to our cheer. There was great news on the
radio: Hitler was dead in Germany and the Allies were
victorious in Europe!

Best of all, my very own calf, April, was growing
and following me around like a pup. I was hurrying to
the barn to tell Grandpa the latest news. I repeated it

over and over as I ran along. "General Eisenhower says the Germans have surrendered. The flags of freedom fly all over Europe."

I knew he'd be in his favorite part of the barn and that's where I spotted his hat above the plank walls of the tool shed. He was great at repairing anything— he had even miraculously gotten the truck engine running again. I blurted out the message. Grandpa went on and on that he was glad to hear the news, but his face held a frown.

"I hate to tell you this, Hopadeedee, but a terrible thing happened a while ago. I was filling this bucket with gasoline from a big barrel and must've overlooked one of those kittens that are always underfoot around here."

"Oh, no!" I knew he couldn't help it. He loved animals just like I did. "I'll get a box and find Celia. She likes to bury things," I answered. As I walked away, I felt sorry that I had not spent more time getting to know the spring kittens. My calf had become my main interest. We were as close as pals could be.

Celia was helping Mama get the brooder ready for the new baby chicks. She only needed to hear the bad news to be ready to dig a tiny grave in the animal cemetery. With all her new grown-up ways, I was glad to see that she still enjoyed being with me sometimes.

We had plotted the animal cemetery last year. It was on a steep bank past our lane, where pretty sand plum bushes grew along the fence row. There was also a clump of small, scraggly catalpa trees that made skimpy afternoon shade.

On that first day we'd buried two yellow chicks, singing over and over, "Just As I Am," a proper Baptist mournful digging song. After hoeing all the weeds in the area, we'd found enough red rocks to make a sort of wall to mark off the cemetery. As we worked, the county road grading machine moved steadily down the road in our direction. Charlie, the grader man, was hired each spring to strip the roadside banks of all the greenery and make the bar ditches deeper at each side of the road, so rainwater would run off the roadbed.

As he'd moved closer, Celia hatched a plan. Just as the huge, noisy machine was within feet of our spot, she and I had walked toward it, waving and carrying a drink of cold, fresh well water in a Mason jar and a bouquet of plum blossoms. We handed both to Charlie. He assured us that he would avoid grading that spot for a long time. Our cemetery would be safe.

Today like always, after sweeping the cemetery clean, we raced to the chicken house. We climbed on top of the tin roof to watch for animal shapes in the clouds, hoping they were a sign of the departed animals' heavenly entry. Celia spotted a kitten-shaped cloud before I was barely settled.

Thunderheads were billowing high in the limitless sky, gathering for the first good spring rain. I breathed in the strong, sweet smell of turned earth. From the roof-top, I could see the red cattle and newborn calves stand-ing far off in the south pasture, poised for the thunder and raindrops.

In the west field, low red dust clouds followed Daddy and the tractor. After working all night at the drill-ing rig, he'd eat breakfast, climb on the Allis-Chalmers tractor, and head for the fields. By four o'clock he'd be back, clean up, eat a little, then fall in bed until Mr. Johnson arrived at nine o'clock to drive back to the oil well. We hardly saw him, but at least we knew he had no time for whiskey at the Blue Moon Saloon. One night as he was leaving for work, he'd announced, "The rough-necks call this the graveyard shift." Celia had answered, "Daddy, you're going to look like a ghost if you keep this up." He'd looked at Mama and winked, "Well, at least I'll be a ghost with some cash money."

Celia and Grandpa tried their best to fill in for Daddy in the fields, but no one could replace his skill in growing cotton.

I watched Daddy's tractor dust drift toward the pasture where trees were leafing in a bright yellow green. A red cardinal flitted above the chicken house roof look-ing for a place to nest.

It seemed signs of spring were everywhere around the farm. Barn swallows were building their odd-shaped nests in the barn. The goldfinch and orioles were resting on their way to places up north, like Montana or Illinois. I'd heard the meadowlark's calling, but Mama's favorite bird, the whippoorwill, never talked until later in the heat of the Oklahoma summer.

Celia and I lingered a while, lying on the warm rippled tin roof, talking about the upcoming overdue trip to town. We were happy that for once Grandpa could not fix something. Mama's wringer washing machine was beyond his tinkering, so a trip to the help-yourself laundry in town was going to have to happen soon.

"I hope we can visit Elmer at the bank," I said. "Think Mama will let us?"

"I don't know. Maybe he'll be at Good's drugstore having lunch. We can look there, and then let's explore the alleys behind Nola's laundry," Celia said.

"Do you think Nola really sleeps on the piles of clothes in the back of the building?" I repeated the rumor I'd heard on the bus.

"Don't ever ask her," Celia said. "You know she won't give us any bubblegum if we don't behave."

*
**

Tiny, stout Nola scared me. She always pinched my check. I thought her gruff voice had a mysterious witch-like quality. She wore thick glasses over big owl eyes and clomped about in men's work boots. She also was the photographer and the typesetter at the weekly county newspaper, which meant that her fingers were permanently black from the ink.

Nola would hug Mama and brag about Sarah, patting my sister as if she were her own daughter. Nola was proud of Sarah. She had published Sarah's photograph in the newspaper along with the story of her winning the highest honor, the Principal's Award, at the all-school assembly. Nola was always quick to quote Mrs. Hopkins's praise at the ceremony: "Sarah's commitment to perfect grades, her exemplary spirit, and courage earned her this annual award." To be honest, it had been a great moment for the whole family, not just Sarah. Celia and I had proudly wormed our way through the crowd to stand right beside her.

We'd needed some pride after the earlier school gossip and bus taunting. On that day we rode home on Elmer's bus a bit more confident. When Elmer shook Sarah's hand and announced how proud he was of her—I beamed, too.

Still cloud watching and daydreaming on the chicken house tin roof, I could picture Nola's laundry, the machines clacking loud, water spilling over the tubs, with the air full of bleach and bluing and soap. Our wet clothes, and Daddy's now-clean oil-field greasers, would ride home in baskets in the back of our truck, to be hung on the clotheslines north of the henhouse. I had watched Mama and Sarah clothespin faster than the wind whipping our wet clothes could dry them. Next, I knew that endless ironing would follow for days, the starched dresses standing up on their own before the hot iron tamed each ruffle and ribbon.

My daydream ended with the drone of the tractor. We waved to Daddy, who was now plowing the field closest to the barnyard. Straight green rows stretched out toward the horizon. The cotton fields lay beside the wheat, and the wheat gave way to fields of corn and then one of red-topped cane. The quiltlike farm was covered with the promise of spring, of new leaves on scrub oak and purple flowers on the lone redbud near the garden. It was a beautiful sight, and it would be even more beautiful when it belonged to us. I was full of hope.

EIGHT

I PRESSED MY NOSE FLAT against the window screen as Sarah turned the radio volume lower. "Why do we have this daylight savings time anyway?" I asked.

"Shhhh, keep your voice down, you know Daddy's trying to catch a little sleep upstairs!"

She was setting the supper table and whispered, "The savings time gives us more daylight hours to work in the evening. You know we need every bit of daylight we can get."

I knew we sure weren't singing along with the radio lately. Daddy still worked the graveyard shift on a rig over in Kingfisher County and had been harvesting wheat every day for over a week. His only rest was sometime in between the two backbreaking jobs.

"This is no time to slide," he'd said at breakfast.

The days were dry and scorching hot. My bare summer feet had celebrated the end of school long enough to develop a thick callous of skin. This helped when I accidentally stepped on a goathead sticker or in a sandbur patch.

I jumped off the front porch, untied April's long rope halter, and headed to the barn where Mama and Grandpa were milking. April was growing bigger and bigger by the day. The small brass neck bell jangled with every step. Mr. Harris had brought me the bell tied on a beautiful blue ribbon when April was just a newborn. He'd said, "It's not every day you get your first pet— or one as special as yours." I'd wanted to hug him, but awkwardly shook his hand instead. Now, the bell seemed tiny—for April had grown up—and become a bull! I had just assumed she was a girl calf. Everyone knew it was impossible to love a bull. But I did.

I had not wanted to believe Grandpa when one day he'd told me she was a bull calf, and I moped all day, and was hurt to the bone when Celia teased, "April's a bull ... April Fool."

"Come on, Maggie," Sarah had cheered me. "I made a fancy movie star dress for you—and I want to photograph you and April by the flower bed."

She'd cut a bouquet of plum blossoms for me to hold, and said, "You look like Miss America, even with your pigtails."

***

At the barn, I pushed the heavy wooden barnyard gate shut and climbed the board fence to secure the latch. It was quieter at milking time ever since Daddy took the extra job. Mama and Grandpa worked silently, never visiting with one another as they did chores—there was too much to do and too little time to do it.

On past summer evenings, Daddy and Mama sometimes sang as they milked. We girls would join in, singing harmony with Daddy's bass and Mama's alto. Those dusky summer evenings were my favorite times, when crickets and locusts called and fireflies danced and the odor of fresh milk mingled with the sweet smell of fried potatoes and onions warming on the kitchen stove. Everyone safe and together.

Once the land was finally ours, I bet every day would feel like those summer evenings.

"Mr. Harris is right. Owning land is the future. If we can buy it, keep my job, and get a little money in the bank, we'll never have to worry again," Daddy said at supper. It was his first optimistic comment in a long time, and I seized it.

But it was a strange comment for Daddy to make, as if he were telling Grandpa Poynter something new and different—something Grandpa'd never heard of. We all knew Grandpa Poynter had bought and lost land time and again all the way from Arkansas to Oklahoma. He just could never seem to keep it.

After supper, we waved goodbye as Daddy climbed into Mr. Johnson's rickety old truck heading to the oil rig. April and I followed Grandpa to Joe and Slim's pen. As Grandpa fed them, the mules swished their long black tails at the nagging flies.

Grandpa looked worried. "These hateful flies could mean rain's coming, Hopadeedee. If it rains, we'll never get the wheat out of the field before I have to go," Grandpa said.

"Can't you stay, Grandpa? We haven't had time to swim in the spring pool or make ice cream or even toad houses!"

"We'll do it yet. What say we take April down to the creek right now and build some toad houses before dark?" he asked.

When we passed the fenced off section of pasture where Old Hitler grazed, Grandpa asked, "What are you planning to do about April, Hop? He's getting too big for a pet."

"Oh, I know it. Everybody warns me, but she's, uh, he's still gentle and sweet. He's not mean like Old Hitler." I looked up at Grandpa. "I can't stop worrying about what to do."

I wanted to cry but didn't. Instead, I turned and faced him, "I can't stand saying goodbye to you or

April. I'm going to miss you, Grandpa. Who will I ever talk to?"

He put his hand on my shoulder. "Oh, Hop, you know April's not mean now, but he is a bull, and there's bound to come a time when you will have to let him be what he is. You're smart. You'll know the right thing to do when you need to do it."

Looking around the shady creek bank, he added, "You're smart about toads too, I see. Were you here today already?"

I nodded. "But we can make some more, Grandpa."

He took off his shoes and socks and joined me on the soft, damp sand.

"Grandpa, your shoes are the oddest things," I said.

"I have so many corns and bunions that I have to cut holes in my shoes to ease my feet," he said, laughing. "Even my dress-up shoes have cutouts here and there."

"I think they look like sandals. You know, someday I'm going to have a pair of sandals, store-bought sandals."

We concentrated on piling the wet sand up over our bare feet and patted it smooth and firm. It was wonderful to smell the musty creek dirt and feel its grittiness between our toes. Slowly, we each inched our feet out of the packed sand, leaving a cave-like house about the size of a large toad where our feet had been.

I looked around the creek, then asked, "Grandpa, do you think we'll get to stay here?" I grasped Grandpa's big tan roughened hand.

"Your Mama and Daddy are doing everything they can, and the rest of us can do nothing but to lend our hands and hope. Your dad is trying to beat his demons, and it looks like he's winning," he said. "Try not to worry so much, Maggie. Let's promise we'll make toad houses right here again next summer."

Maggie. My real-life name, he said it! I smiled and wondered if he thought I was getting too old for a nickname. He saw my surprise and hollered, "Hopadeedee and toad houses!"

The summer sounds surrounded us as dusk fell. Brilliant little bugs hurtled across the top of the spring water. The distant laughter of Celia and Sarah, in a rare moment of playing hide-and-seek in the tall cotton, moved across the pasture. A mournful whippoorwill called goodnight, and nearby I clearly heard the gentle bawl of a spring calf-turned bull.

I felt a sudden chill. I knew I was losing April. Maybe not now, but someday.

NINE

AT BREAKFAST, WHEN MAMA ANNOUNCED our second trip to town in two weeks, I jumped around the kitchen squealing.

"You sound just like a baby pig," Celia said.

Sarah asked, "May we go to the library this time, please?"

"And Good's Drug Store," I added, glaring at Celia.

Mama nodded. "We have other places to go, too."

Mama's big plan for the trip to town was to collect the final payment for our wheat crop at the co-op and keep enough cash to pay the few workers chopping cotton alongside Grandpa and Daddy in our fields. She'd open a bank account with the rest of the money. A bank account with money saved toward buying the farm!

From the co-op we headed to the Farmers and Merchants' Bank. I was excited to see Elmer, but a little nervous too. The bank was spacious and beautiful. The black and white marble floor glistened in the sunshine and the bank tellers' cages with iron bars over the openings seemed solemn and important.

Elmer jumped up from behind his desk, flashing his warm smile. A handsome man in a fancy suit and tie came toward us nodding hello. Elmer introduced us and said that Mr. Hopkins was the president of the bank. He added, "Girls, his wife is your school superintendent —Mrs. Hopkins, you already know her very well." Mr. Hopkins smiled, "I've heard about you smart girls from my wife as well as Elmer. She sure loves that school, and it appears you do too."

We were so quiet you could hear a pin drop. I had been holding my breath because I was afraid we didn't belong here.

I was proud to be in this place and proud to know Elmer. It seemed like we were rich, just having a real bank account. Elmer counted out the money and Mama signed an important looking paper and got a small passbook. Then Elmer reached into a bottom drawer and pulled out three small piggy banks. He said, "Girls, when these little banks are full, bring them back, and I'll help you each open your own account." He smiled at me and patted my hand, "I'm sure glad to see you, Maggie." Then he turned to Mama, almost whispering, he added some encouragement. "I hear Arley is working day and night. Looks like everything is going smooth, Lou."

I watched him as he shook Mama's hand. He was gentle and kind, but businesslike, too. I guess being a banker meant you had to be quiet. How did he put up with our noisy bus? I stared at Elmer, thinking that when the cotton harvest was over, we'd be back on the school bus with him. He was a hero. We all knew that. Mr. Harris had told us that Elmer won his medals on D-Day, at Omaha Beach, when the allies invaded France, the biggest fight of its kind in all of history. He was on a landing craft that was pummeled by German guns. Many of our soldiers died or were wounded—but Elmer and the remaining crew delivered our soldiers to the fight and carried the injured back to our ships. He never talked about his own wounds. He put others ahead of himself then, just as he did today. A hero. My hero too.

*
**

Later, in the hot truck, Sarah and Celia were trying to remember the words to the song we'd heard in Good's Drug Store:

> Mairzy doats
> and dozy doats,
> and liddle lamzy divey.
> A kiddley divey too,
> wouldn't you?

We'd laughed and laughed too loud in the high-backed booth. We laughed so loud the soda jerk had glanced our way and frowned. But who cared? All our real worries seemed distant as we licked our ice cream and sang along with the cheery song.

I had chosen banana ice cream but was now sorry. My tummy was uneasy. Still, I was happy. With library books, ice cream, a visit to Elmer's bank, and now buying a block of real ice, it had been a near perfect summer day.

I kneeled on the stack of library books we'd gotten, watching the iceman through the rear window. From the floor of the ice dock, he threw a fifty-pound block of ice into our truck bed. When we reached home, Mama and Sarah would use ice hooks to lift whatever was left of this rare luxury into the top of our metal icebox.

After the ice dock, Mama made a quick stop at the five-and-ten store. "Supplies," she said. "Wait here." We didn't ask her what was in the brown sack when she climbed back into the truck and turned from Main Street driving west into a neighborhood I had never seen. The houses were unpainted, but the dirt yards were swept clean. Mama stopped at a small house enclosed by a cobbled-up fence. As she approached the gate, a little girl ran to meet her.

Mama said, "Please give this envelope to your Daddy—now, make sure you do. He'll be looking for it. I'm certain."

When she returned to the truck she was smiling. "Well, at least we got the hired cotton choppers paid."

A few streets over Sarah pointed to a red brick building. "That's Douglass School," she said. "They have a gymnasium, but we don't. Our basketball team practices there."

"Who goes to school there?" I asked.

Sarah pointed to some Negro kids playing in the street and said, "They do. They have their own school, and we have our own. But Mrs. Loper says someday we'll all go to school together."

"That will be a long time coming, and probably not without a fight," Mama said. "This part of town is where our cotton workers live, Maggie."

Some of the kids started running beside the truck,

and when they stopped, I waved back at them as if I knew them. I wondered if I'd ever see them again.

Turning a corner, Mama slowed the truck to a crawl in front of a long building that looked like a worn-out barn, with a skinny porch over one wide window and a single glass door. Overgrown grass grew alongside the shacklike building and the bare dirt area in front led up to three steps. Someone had drawn a crescent-shaped moon and scrawled crude letters in bright blue paint, BOOTS BLUE MOON, on the wall above the entry.

The truck jerked as Mama shifted into low gear to move on past the deserted looking building.

I was curious but confused. I'd heard Sarah talking about Daddy going to Boots's. But why would Daddy ever go to such a scary-looking place?

I turned to Sarah, "Is that the place where Daddy goes when he doesn't come home to us—the place where he gets that awful whiskey?"

Sarah nodded, touching my hand. Mama kept her eyes on the road, and Celia just stared out the window.

"Well, he hasn't been there in a while," I said, "He's been working too hard."

Everyone was silent as we bumped along the weed-lined road where little shantylike houses sprang up here and there. It dawned on me now what the WHITE ONLY signs at the movie theater and at Pfrimmer's Café meant.

Once past the train depot and Jack's gas station, we turned onto our road. Enormous layers of thunderheads were building in the eastern sky. I glanced back at town and watched as the melting block of ice left a tiny trail of water in the red dirt.

My tummy ached, rolling from the rich banana ice cream, but worse than that, my head rumbled with worry about a blue crescent moon on a spooky shack in town.

Mama helped me into the house, bathed my face and feet, and laid out a pallet of pretty quilts in the front parlor between the open windows and screen door in hopes there would be a breeze.

"I'll bring some chipped ice and sprinkle the pallet with water, so you'll feel cooler," Mama said. "You've had a long day."

It was burning hot, and thunderheads rumbled near as the sky became overcast. I heard rain crows sounding off near the creek.

Much later, I woke smelling fresh rain and saw everyone sitting on the front porch, enjoying the cooler air.

"Summer rains are spotty," Daddy said as he was leaving for his night work. "The shower barely touched the Victory Garden, girls."

"I hope you're right," said Grandpa. "I was planning to dig the potatoes tomorrow. Old Joe and Slim'll earn their keep for sure." He turned toward me. "Are you going to help me, Hopadeedee?"

I nodded, slipping onto his lap. But I made a face when he teased, "I'll buy you some banana ice cream if you'll help."

∗∗

I ran outside before daybreak, when I heard Joe and Slim's jangly harness. They were plodding uphill toward the garden. Grandpa guided a plow behind the mules, which were bound together with worn harness leather. Teddy led the procession.

Mama, my sisters, and I wore our oldest clothes and shoes and waited beside bushel baskets. The dark morning was already hot and humid from the rain.

With a flick of a worn leather rein and a whistle, the mules strained forward. Grandpa waded behind the first spiraling furrow, stepping around the exposed potatoes. Then I called, "I see car lights. Daddy's coming!"

Daddy headed straight to the garden to help. He made those same clucking noises, like gee and haw, and low whistles we'd heard last winter in the big snowstorm. It was his special mule talk, and as the earth rolled out behind the plow, it unearthed a sea of potatoes. We girls followed, tossing potato after potato into bushel baskets, leaving each heavy basket wherever it became full so Mama and Grandpa could carry them down into the cellar. They'd become our winter meals and seed potatoes next February.

When Celia complained, "My back hurts. We've picked up enough potatoes for five years," I groaned, too.

The sun was high in the sky before Mama finally yelled, "Biscuits! Come wash up!"

During breakfast, Mama announced, "We're having a party. We're going to have a big early supper for Grandpa. He leaves tonight for Uncle Fred's in the Rio Grande Valley. Mr. Johnson and Daddy will drive him to the train depot."

Even though I was sad that Grandpa was leaving, getting ready for a party was fun. It seemed as if we cooked all afternoon. We made potato salad and deviled eggs and pulled husks and silk from a dozen ears of field corn. Mama made her famous two-crust apple pie and an angel food cake that stood at least eight inches tall. The ice cream custard was cooked and cooling. Grandpa himself would crank the ice cream freezer.

"Now I know why we got the ice," I said, hugging Mama.

Late that afternoon, an unfamiliar green car turned into the lane. The man who climbed out and walked up to the house introduced himself. "I'm John Thurston, from the government Farm Security Administration.

I've come to see how you're doing. Think you'll be able to pay off your loan with us?"

I ran to stand next to Mama and heard him politely accept Mama's invitation to stay for the party. I was horrified! Here was the man I feared. The one who "tells about farming from behind a desk." He could keep us from having the farm—and Mama wanted to feed him!

Daddy waved as he came in from the field and pulled the tractor near the shed. He and Mr. Thurston spent a long time walking in the fields inspecting the cotton and grain. When they came to the pasture to count the calves and cows, Teddy, April and I met them. I was proud to hear Daddy say, "That calf belongs to Maggie."

⁑

We moved the oak table and chairs to the front yard and into the shade of the house. Mama used a pretty tablecloth and her best glasses. It was a wonderful supper. The food was so tasty, Mr. Thurston ate like a starving man. We listened closely as the men discussed the war and spoke of our new president, Harry Truman.

"He's a Missouri fellow—good stock—knows this part of the country well. And he's tough as nails," Grandpa said.

"Yes, he's going to outsmart the Japanese soon." Mr. Thurston said it as if he had some special inside information. Maybe he did, since he was in the government.

After supper, I sat on top of the wooden ice cream tub to hold it still while grandpa cranked the handle. There was a thick gunny sack covering the ice and salt, but it still felt wonderfully cold. Celia and I each sucked on a piece of the salty ice. Finally, when the handle was impossible to turn any further, Grandpa added more salt and covered the ice with more gunny sacks, so the ice cream would firm up.

Turning from the freezer, Grandpa held up the mysterious brown sack from town. He grinned as he pulled a white leather softball from the sack, and said, "Okay, let's play ball!"

Celia and I grabbed Grandpa's hands, cheering and shouting. "Thank you!" We'd played softball all summer with a homemade ball of wound-up string. It worked, but it sure was heavy. And it sure didn't have that wonderful leathery smell of a real ball.

Grandpa grinned from ear to ear and winked at Mama. Then he and Daddy chose up sides. The game was certain to be uneven—with me, Grandpa and frail-looking Mr. Thurston against Daddy, Sarah, and Celia. Mama said she wanted to be the all-time catcher.

At first, Grandpa pitched, but they hit his every throw, and it wasn't long before Daddy's team was ahead. When Mr. Thurston said he'd take a turn at pitching, I almost groaned aloud. We'd be sure to lose now. But in no time Mama was calling the score: 3 up and 3 down. Tied!

"Batter up," she called. Grandpa winked at me, "Hop, you go first. And hit for the cedar trees. Never a doubt!" he yelled, sounding just like Daddy.

I hit that new leather ball over the trees and ran all three bases before Celia found it and threw it to Daddy.

We were all yelling and whooping. I even hugged Mr. Thurston after he hit a long drive past Sarah, bringing Grandpa in to score, too.

In the next round, Daddy hit a homer, and Celia scored on a ground ball I couldn't reach.

We were behind, but I knew I could hit another homer. I was ready at home plate. This time Celia was pitching. She frowned in concentration, pulled her arm back as far as she could, and threw that new shiny softball full speed, straight into my open mouth.

I fell, both hands trying to catch the blood streaming from my lips. I could feel my two front baby teeth dangling from my gums, then ran half-sobbing to the windmill where April was tied.

"Look at me, little tough-nut," Daddy pleaded when he reached me.

"Open your mouth, Maggie, I want to see how loose your teeth are."

"No," I shook my head firmly, burrowing into April's neck.

Grandpa and Mama urged me to let him look. I shook my head no, as Mama handed me her apron to sop up the blood running down my chin.

Celia looked at me horrified. "Maggie, I'm sorry—that new ball just flew out of my hand. I never meant to hit you."

Sarah, on the other side of April, reached over to stroke my hair. April stood as still as a statue even though he was surrounded by everyone. Through my tears I could see Mr. Thurston, standing apart but watching closely.

I was hurting. I could feel my teeth dangling in all the gummy blood. I didn't dare swallow, I just let the blood run out the sides of my mouth. I was about to choke when Daddy reappeared with his leather razor strap in one hand. "If you don't let me look in your mouth and check those teeth, I'll have to spank you. I don't want you to swallow them."

"I don't care," I blubbered.

"Then I'll spank April until you let me see those teeth."

That did it. I knew he meant business. No one would harm April.

I opened my mouth and in one gentle pull, Daddy suddenly had both teeth in his fingers. I was startled and

I ran my tongue over my gums feeling for the teeth. The empty spaces and gummy blood caused me to giggle. We moved toward the house, Mama's arms around me, then she worked to flush all the blood from my mouth. Once my cleaned teeth were admired by all, I held them in my hand, turning them over and over—wondering if they were big enough for the tooth fairy to leave me something if I put them under my pillow.

We dawdled over Grandpa's delicious, sweet ice cream, and as dusk moved up the hill from the creek, it was time to bid Mr. Thurston goodbye. He turned to me and smiled. "Maggie, I always want to be on your team."

I grinned. My toothless smile must've looked funny because before I knew it, Mr. Thurston picked me up and swung me in a circle—like an old friend.

Then, he shook Daddy's hand, "Your cotton is the best I've seen in these parts. It will bring top dollar, Arley. And I bet the sale of your cows plus the cotton will be enough to pay off your loan. I'll personally arrange for the sale of the cattle following the cotton harvest."

I swelled at Mr. Thurston's words. I thought I might pop, I was so thrilled. It seemed almost too good to be true.

Grandpa made a little speech. "Sometimes, it's not easy to tell the good times from the hard times until you look back. But I know that these are good times, girls, and I'm happy to have been here with each of you." Then he tweaked my pigtail and laughed, "We had some bloody good fun, didn't we, Hopadeedee?"

The next morning, I was amazed to find a rare silver dollar under my pillow from the tooth fairy. I held it and studied it a long time before slipping it into the piggy bank that Elmer had given me. But, once downstairs, I saw that my tooth fairy wish had not come true. Grandpa Poynter had left for Texas in the night. He was somewhere on the train heading south. I imagined him in his black frock coat with his FDR button on the lapel and his funny looking cut out dress shoes. I missed him already.

I wished I'd had the chance to talk to him about Boots's Blue Moon. I needed to ask Grandpa why his son would choose such a scary place over our farmhouse and us. What if Daddy decided to go there again?

TEN

"IT'S A FEAST!" EXCLAIMED GRANDMA Judy-Bob Pate, clapping her hands as we placed Mama's yeast rolls, my hand-churned butter, and Sarah's freshly baked blackberry pies on Aunt Polly's long dinner table. Mismatched platters and bowls filled with sliced tomatoes, corn on the cob, potatoes, green peas, and crispy fried chicken completely covered every inch of the table.

Bounty from summer gardens had come from near and far. Aunts and cousins had balanced lidded dishes and pies covered with tea towels on their laps as aging trucks and cars rattled along dusty roads heading for the Pate family reunion.

I wished Daddy had come, too. But he never came to

these reunions. I knew he didn't get along with Mama's family. Mama always reminded us that Grandma Judy-Bob and Daddy were friends. It was Mama's papa, Grandpa Jessie, who didn't approve of Daddy or his drinking. "After all," Sarah whispered, "Grandpa Jessie is Great-Grandma Caroline Pate's stubborn son and set in his Indian ways."

He resembled Great-Grandma Caroline too, who was sinewy and stately with her fierce black eyes. Whenever we went to his house, I always stared at a photograph of her in Grandpa's bedroom. Had she ever had any fun or laughed? Grandpa's own serious face wore Caroline's lifelong message: take the next step, finish what you start, overcome anything.

His success following her example was clear in his gnarled hands. We cousins were a little afraid of him, and only Grandma Judy could make him smile. Mama was their firstborn and Grandpa's favorite by a mile. But Grandpa had no respect for the Poynter bunch Mama had married into and little patience for weakness or quitters. There was unsettled business in Grandpa's heart.

Earlier, along the road to Aunt Polly and Uncle Albert's farm, Mama had cautioned us, "Don't mention Daddy's fight in town or the fire to anyone—especially now. He's doing so much better, don't you think?" I nodded, but Sarah and Celia were silent.

As our noon dinner began, ominous dark clouds

began rolling around the hilltop farmhouse. After we ate, my cousins and I decided we would play hide-and-seek in Uncle Albert's huge barn. We played hard and fast, swinging from the barn rafters, diving into the straw, hiding behind posts and between bales of hay in every nook and cranny of the stifling hot barn.

When Grandma Judy-Bob called us in for dessert and the singing, we followed her up the hillside, glad for pie and Aunt Evelyn's ice cream. The skies were dark as night as we kids sprawled near the piano on the cool linoleum floor. Aunt Polly was plunking out Mama's favorite song, so we joined in, singing the last refrain.

> When my blue moon
> turns to gold again,
> and the rainbow
> turns the clouds away—
> when my blue moon
> turns to gold again,
> I'll be back within
> your arms to stay.

We kids clapped and hooted, settling down for the familiar songs like: "In the Good Old Summertime," "Shine on Harvest Moon," and Grandma's all-time best hymn, "Trust and Obey." The reunion singalongs always ended after Grandma played her French harp and jigged along to an old-timey mountain tune. When we saw she'd made Grandpa smile, everyone laughed and hugged.

The dark and stormy reunion day was ending on a good note until Uncle Albert brought up the war. He stood up. "I waited until we'd all had a good time today to tell you some terrible news that we'll likely remember for a long time." We kids grew quiet and inched closer to the grownups.

"Our country dropped a bomb on a place in Japan called Hiroshima," he said, "It's a new kind of bomb, atomic, they call it, supposed to be the most destructive ever."

He paused. "The radio said thousands of people most likely would be killed or be burned by the blast." Then he added, "You may recall that President Truman warned the Japanese to surrender or be ruined by air and you all know how tough he is. I reckon Harry gave it to 'em alright."

Uncle Gordon broke the quiet, "Do you think that'll help finally end the war?"

Uncle Albert shook his head, "I don't know—it's gone on so long, I guess we're all used to it. But this bomb really is a different sort of fight. I'm sure praying for the war to end, and not get worse."

The scary war talk was frightening, even though I didn't understand all of it. Suddenly it seemed as if everything in the world was scary and sad. Everything but my calf, April.

Just then an enormous clap of thunder sounded as a streak of lightning lit up the dark room. "Don't like the sound of that," Uncle Gordon said, peering out the window. "Bet we're in for a hellacious storm. The Old Farmer's Almanac predicted late summer would bring unusual weather!"

"I'm worried sick about rain, too much would ruin the cotton harvest. Remember in 1932 when all the cotton rotted in the field?" Uncle Albert said.

"Yeah, and then just three years later when the winds and the dusters rolled in and no rain fell for years," added Uncle Gordon throwing up his hands. "Weather—it can make or break us."

I couldn't stand hearing any more negative talk. The possibility of Daddy's cotton rotting was the last straw. I pulled at Mama and whispered, "Let's go Mama, now?"

Again, streaks of lightning cut the dark sky, thunder rolling nearby.

Mama nodded. Already gathering our pans and bowls, she said, "Polly, it's sure been fun, but we need to get home before the Farmer's Almanac storm of the century hits." She winked. Some other folks began collecting their bowls and platters, too.

Our goodbyes and hugs were interrupted by two

long rings, one short ring, then again, two long rings, one short. It was Aunt Polly's party line telephone.

"Yes, Lou's still here. Let me get her." Holding the earpiece against her chest, Aunt Polly turned to Mama. "It's Arley, from Mr. Harris's house."

I saw Mama's back stiffen. She grabbed the wall phone as if for strength. "On no," she whispered. "We're leaving now. We're on our way. We'll beat the storm."

She hung the telephone receiver on its hook. Turning back to us, I saw the worry in her eyes. "The war got Daniel Harris. Nadeen rode to our place to get Daddy to help with Mr. Harris. Arley said, 'He's gone wild.'"

Within minutes, our old truck was banging and bumping up and down the rocky hills, only slowing in the sandy stretches. "If the storm breaks along this pitiful sand and clay road, we'll never make it to the Harrises'," said Sarah.

"Getting stuck in mud would be the last straw," Mama agreed, pressing down on the gas pedal as the black sky closed in on us.

A zigzag of lightning ran across the horizon and crackling thunder followed.

"This is a going-to-the-cellar storm," yelled Celia. "I can feel it."

We'd seen Oklahoma storms bluster up for an

entire day, then suddenly change direction, taking the teasing rain with it. Or the sky might build high white thunderheads that turned yellowish black and green, running every living thing into hiding underground.

I stood, holding onto the dashboard, leaning against Sarah's legs, as hot wind and stinging sand hit my face. I knew Daddy was watching the clouds and worrying about rain on the cotton. I rubbed my dirty hands against my eyes to clear the tears when Mama said, "Poor, sweet Mr. Harris. All his dreams destroyed by the storm of war."

"Look! Fire flaming up above the treetops," Sarah yelled, "It's at the Balsingers'."

"That lightning strike probably hit an outbuilding," Mama said. "Hope it's not the house."

I remembered the awful night of our own fire and how lucky we were to squelch it before it took the whole house.

Finally, Mama turned the final bend in the road and boiled the dust for the last mile toward the Harrises' lane of cedars.

"We've outrun the storm!" I cheered.

From Mr. Harris's hill, we could see the Balsingers' barn burning, the gray smoke rolling up and mixing with the green-black clouds.

"I hope they got the horses out," Celia said.

"And the cattle," I added, thinking of April.

We stood staring at the damage even after the hail-stones began falling.

From the porch, Daddy waved at us to hurry toward the musty cellar and safety, just as the storm, with all its fury, broke overhead.

Once inside, we huddled together as the violent wind sucked at the cellar door so that it strained against its hinges. Daddy stood on the steps, struggling to hold onto the handle with all his strength to keep the doors from flying off. In the dimness, Mama moved to Mr. Harris, taking his hands into hers and kneeling in front of him. Even in the fading light of the cellar, I could see that Mr. Harris's watery blue eyes were hollow. Mournful.

I watched the hem of Mama's dress soaking up water that was quickly rising on the dirt floor. The noise of this storm was eerie. Different. It was a weird whistlelike sound—so loud I could barely hear the wailing and sobbing of Ruby and Nadeen. Suddenly, Mr. Harris, clutching the War Department telegram, began shaking it in anger toward the noisy heavens.

The dank smell of mildew and the long bench pressed against the cellar wall was like being in our church basement. I thought the storm's loud noise sounded a lot like Reverend Perkins's hellfire and brimstone preaching, too.

Rainwater spilled down the cellar walls and the

lantern flickered, as I edged closer to Sarah, who sat perched on the edge of the potato-drying table. I closed my eyes and listened as she hummed Grandma's favorite hymn. The roaring wind, odd whistling noise, and loud banging sounds were terrifying.

Then suddenly the hail ceased, the rain lessened, and small bits of sunlight shone through the cracks of the cellar doors. The quarreling wind was over in a flash, and finally, Daddy pushed the doors back and we climbed the muddy steps up into daylight.

Near the house, huge limbs were broken off trees, and a few cedar trees had simply disappeared from the row at the lane. There were boards and shingles everywhere. A big piece of the barn roof was missing, and telephone poles lay crooked, even though they were still tethered to the sagging lines. But, I wondered, what were the big wet green and white mounds lying all around?

Picking up a soggy wet mass of it, Daddy said in disbelief, "It's cotton. I think it's *our* cotton. Blown all this way."

Daddy's eyes were full of worry, his forehead furrowed, but he stayed strong for Mr. Harris. How could he complain? He'd lost cotton. Mr. Harris had lost a son.

As I watched, Daddy put his arm around Mr. Harris's shoulders, whispered to him, and with an awkward handshake said goodbye. I saw Mama and Daddy's eyes lock in understanding. We would stay to help the

Harrises, but Daddy must go immediately. He needed to find out how much destruction had struck our farm.

What if the storm had taken all our precious cotton? It would be the end of our dream. It would be the end of Daddy. I was heartbroken at the sight of him striking out across the muddy, open field, stalks of wet cotton cradled in his arms.

ELEVEN

BY DUSK, MAMA AND SARAH had prepared a warm meal, but Mr. Harris hardly touched his plate. He and Mama quietly discussed the uncertainty of when or how Daniel's body would be returned and if Mama could drive him to town to find out. He cried openly, pounding the table with his fist. Ruby and Nadeen's sobbing and his grieving sent Celia and me out into the drenched, littered yard.

We poked about the debris near the barn corral. Celia whistled to Mr. Harris's horses, patting them when they moved close.

"Think we should feed them?" she said.

"Yes, let's find their oats. I sure hope Daddy feeds

April. I wonder if he's okay. What if our barn fell in during the storm?"

"Most likely Daddy's just checking on the cotton."

"Do you think we lost it?"

"I'm afraid," she gestured to the wreckage all around us, "it's likely. But we'll know soon enough."

The next day, after it seemed we had prepared enough food for the Harrises for a month, we left their place and headed home, dreading what we might find there.

The tires spun around and around in the deep red mud. Finally, halfway between the Harrises' place and our farmhouse, we just gave up. We left the truck with its wheels buried, and with our shoes in hand, we walked barefoot toward home in ankle-deep mud.

From the lane, the house and barn roofs appeared undamaged. There was a single blade missing from the windmill. Tree limbs were broken in the cedar thicket, and the yard was covered with leaves and sticks, most likely from the creek trees. But everything seemed to have survived.

Then Mama spied her hen house. She stopped short, her mouth falling open. The tin roof was missing and some of the nests were, too. Yet it looked as if every one of her chickens stood huddled within the chicken house. Mama smiled. "How in the world did they keep from blowing away?"

We saw Teddy and Daddy in the distance, on the edge of the west cotton field, the early evening sunset glowing behind them. Daddy raised a hand and started moving in our direction, while Teddy raced lickety-split for us.

As Daddy came closer, Mama rushed to him and put her arms around him. I watched as tears formed and she began to cry. They stood without speaking. I could see his blue eyes were flat. I looked beyond him and saw why. Row after row of cotton. Wrecked.

We girls turned away, but not before we realized all we'd lost. It wasn't just the cotton. The silent and awful truth came through. We'd lost Daddy.

*
**

My heart pounding, I turned and ran to the barn, with Teddy and Celia right behind me. Tree limbs and roof shingles lay about the corral, but the big barn and sheds seemed to have miraculously missed serious damage.

"April's in his stall," I yelled. "He's okay, Celia. He just wants outside!" He made an odd noise and bounced toward me, all eyes and ears, as I opened the gate. Here was my loyal, grateful friend.

In the two days I'd been gone so much had changed—it felt good to know that April was still the same.

Later when we all gathered in the kitchen, the room felt too small for all our emotions. Everyone stayed busy, but when supper was ready at last and the glasses were full of milk, we finally had to look at one another. There was no chatter, no words to fill the emptiness. The long quiet was interrupted only by a utensil on a plate or a glass landing on the tabletop.

In the past two days, loss had surrounded us. Finally, Mama staring at her plate, reached out for our hands and looking at each of us, she spoke, "It's overwhelming to see all that work gone in a flash of nature. But somehow we lived through worse times, and we never once considered leaving then. We can't now. We won't. Something good will happen. I know it will. Maybe the remaining cotton crop will be more than we expect. The cows and calves could bring more, too. We'll go meet Mr. Thurston and talk it over. It'll be okay. You'll see."

I wanted to believe her. I did believe her. But then I looked at Daddy. I saw the look of desperation in his face. Working both jobs had exhausted him, and now the loss from the storm had pulled him under. I could see the tiredness sliding down his sloped shoulders. I knew he would never ask for help from Mr. Thurston, nor, I expected, could Mr. Thurston grant it if he wanted to. Even I understood the loan payment was a government decision, with an established deadline and no options. We faced an overwhelming hurdle. Time was not on our side.

In the hot summer night I shivered, as if a cold wind blew through the kitchen conjuring up the memory of the fire and pencil whittling, when I'd felt most afraid and hopeless. My sinking feeling grew until the room seemed the same as before, uncertain and out of control. This worry felt like a rocky road with no end.

*

Daddy quit his night job. He wasn't himself anymore. He either stayed in the barn all day or roamed the creek and pasture. One time, I found him tipsy in the tool shed. I touched his hand, and he silently patted my head. It was as if we both knew that he wanted to explain how badly he felt about his drinking, but he didn't know how. I wanted to hold his big hand and say, "You are Daddy. You are Doak . . . everyone's favorite ball player. Don't you remember how strong you were? Please, Daddy. Please be Doak again. We'll all help; please don't drink anymore." But I saw his shambling gait and his lifeless face, and I could not say the words.

In a voice as soft as feathers, Daddy mumbled, "I am lost."

I knew he was giving up and turning his heart away from our dream.

Over the next few days, signs of neglect rode all over him. His walk grew unsteady, his clothes were soiled, his work sloppy and unfinished. His heart wasn't in it. It didn't seem to be in anything. Shame seemed to cover him like a blanket, and more and more I could smell the sharp odor of whiskey when I was near him. He would not talk or eat. "Where does he get the whiskey bottles?" Celia asked one night. Sarah whispered, "Mama thinks Mr. Johnson has a creek hooch, or maybe Daddy still has an old stash from his nights at Boots's Blue Moon."

One afternoon I saw Mama, Sarah, and Celia gathered at the table studying the calendar discussing how long it would take to harvest the remaining cotton. I moved to listen.

Mama clasped her hands in a tight fist, "All right, I'm determined we're going to move forward—with or without his help. There's a lot more cotton than we first thought—and that's the good news. I don't know how, but we'll figure out a way to get that cotton out of the field. We can do it—I know we can."

We clung to Mama's never-ending optimistic words, but her sad face told a different story. I could see she was agonizing over Daddy's lack of willpower, and I heard worry behind her words. But Mama's strong mouth was set, her black eyes, like Great-Grandmother Caroline's, were intense.

I remembered Grandma Judy-Bob telling us how Mama had resisted Grandpa Pate's warning and married

Daddy anyway. Grandma said the family had gossiped. "Oh yes, they loved the ballgames and had had pride and enthusiasm for him, our very own amazing ballplayer, but when times got bad, they seemed to forget what Arley had been like before. It hurt your mama when they turned against your daddy. When that truck accident happened and he started his slow slide to failure, they quit admiring him. He was banished from the Pate family."

"Your mama's life became one of making ends meet. Her eagerness to help Arley meant she began working side by side in the fields. Their love was such that nothing could ever kill it; it came back time and again, even though they struggled. There was nothing anyone could do to change her mind about your daddy."

Grandma's recollection had helped me understand why Mama never quit believing in Daddy. She'd seen him brave and capable and by sticking by him she dreamed he'd be that way again. She'd make it happen—no matter what.

She thought he could hit another long ball in a different game. While her love was undiminished by events and age, even I saw that Mama's dream and uncommon love was not working now. She could not turn him around.

*
**

On a sizzling morning before the cotton picking began, Mama told us she'd promised to drive Mr. Harris and his girls to Oklahoma City to visit their mother in the sanatorium. Mr. Harris dreaded telling his wife about Daniel's death. Clearly, he knew it was sure to be a difficult day. When they got to our place, Ruby and Nadeen jumped from the car, begging Mama to let us girls go with them. Mr. Harris stood by as Nadeen began to cry. Grabbing Mama's hand, she pled, "We need to have friends with us. It's awful at that place, Mrs. Poynter. Please. Ruby and I won't be so upset if we have the girls."

Mama glanced at the barn. "I can't leave Arley by himself."

"Maybe just Sarah could go then," Mr. Harris said, looking toward the barn, too.

Mama hesitantly nodded okay. I knew she understood their distress.

Celia and I were disappointed not to go, but I felt important as Mama gave us specific instructions before leaving. Celia was to plow the far west field, and I was to take her water and lunch. But my main job would be the hardest. I was to keep an eye on Daddy.

It was well after lunch when Teddy and I followed Daddy to the creek. I watched him search for hidden whiskey bottles in tree trunks and along the red rocks near the spring. When he found an empty bottle, he'd pitch it as far as he could, sometimes almost falling down from the effort of the toss. As his search became more futile, his anger became more vocal. I watched him become "too big" again.

He started up the hill toward the barn and I heard him threatening he would "go to the Blue Moon." Hurrying behind him, I took a shortcut to the tool-shed gate. From there, I quickly ran to the truck shed and snatched the keys, hiding them in my pants pocket. Staying low to the ground, I crept back through the barn and came out of the milking room behind Daddy. He was yelling and kicking the truck because of the missing keys. He crashed into the tool shed, took a hammer and wrenches, and began banging the barn walls and the cultivator, which sat near the shed. He cursed the government and the bank and the truck. He even cursed Teddy.

Suddenly I heard the tractor coming closer. Celia pulled nearer the barnyard. I watched as she reached the field gate and saw Daddy's condition and my undisguised fear. As it registered, I saw her face become full of disgust. I guessed that while she was plowing row after row anger had settled in Celia's heart. Now, the feelings she'd kept inside came streaming out of her. She jumped from the tractor, confronting him, "Damn you, why don't you leave us alone. We're doing all the work and all you do is hurt us. You quit. You quit everything. Even us. We don't need you!"

The air grew so quiet you could hear the horseflies swarming inside the barn. Daddy just stood there, his overalls buttoned crooked, appearing to look straight through her.

"I hate you!" Celia screamed over her shoulder as she stomped toward the house, a confused Teddy following at her heels.

Daddy stood squinting after Celia, his face full of hurt. I felt weak-kneed and heartsick; I wanted to say something—anything—that would remove this heaviness. But the silence was so loud it settled on the barn cats and raced across the rail fence, filling the farm with unhappiness. He stumbled once, the smell of whiskey staggering behind him into the barn.

The sun played games through the open barn doors, lighting up the stalls and a lazy cat here and there. I moved noiselessly past the milking room and into the feed and tack room, trying to follow Daddy. It was my job to stay near him today, to keep my eye on the worry. I had to somehow help him. But how?

I heard a noise in the nearby tool shed and quietly moved to a hole in the wall to peer inside. He had found another bottle. We both realized at the same moment that it, too, was empty. He wavered. Then crashing outside the shed, he opened the gate to Old Hitler's pen and threw the empty bottle straight at the bull's head.

Old Hitler stared at an unrecognizable wild man and began moving his feet nervously in the dirt.

I moved to the open gate, "Daddy, get out of the pen!" But he only walked closer to the bull, shaking his arms and spitting out nonsense.

Suddenly Teddy appeared. Forgetting his fear of the bull, Teddy began barking—a warning plea for Daddy.

But it was too late. The enormous bull spun with a tornado-like force, rearing straight toward Daddy. His huge head and one of his sharp horns scooped him up in the air like a toothpick. Old Hitler kept turning, his horn stuck in Daddy. Finally, Daddy fell to the ground, blood rushing over the dirty hay.

Old Hitler snorted and plodded to the far corner, eyeing Daddy. Daddy, who lay silent on the pen floor.

I couldn't breathe. I couldn't get my arms to move. I couldn't speak or yell. I started shaking. Teddy was gone now. Was Daddy dead? How could I get him out of the pen?

Then I heard Celia's low, courageous voice, "Let's pull him out of here." I looked up from where I had fallen next to Daddy. Celia and I dragged Daddy by his overall straps, trying to keep his head above the hay and dirt. He was barely breathing. We inched toward the gate, leaving a path of blood behind.

Old Hitler stared at us but never moved.

Finally, we were through the gate. Celia slung it shut behind us. We moved together through the big barn, then the milking room, and out into the yard, scarcely able to believe what was happening.

Then without missing a beat, Celia barked orders, "Maggie, get sheets. Get all the bedsheets—and hurry!"

She ran to the truck, then screamed at me, "The keys! Where are the keys?"

I ran with all my might and yelled, "In my pocket. I've got them in my pocket!" I raced back with every sheet I could find, then watched as Celia carried two wide boards from the workshop. She set the boards against the truck bed and motioned me to help push.

Up the boards we pushed Daddy. Blood rushed from his body. His limp arms flailed, and his eyes rolled open and closed. Finally, Celia jumped up into the truck bed and pulled him over the top of the boards as I pushed from below, until he was on the flat bed. Next, we stuffed sheets into the bloodiest parts of his ripped-up overalls.

I leaned over Daddy trying to soothe him while Celia frantically tried to get the truck starter to catch. "Damn you," Celia muttered for the second time in her eleven years.

"Can't you start it?" I yelled.

Celia turned. "I've watched Mama and Daddy start this truck a million times, I'm just praying it's like driving a tractor." Finally, the motor caught. Celia backed the truck out of the tight shed and barreled down the lane with Teddy barking and running alongside.

Celia pushed the truck to its limit. It rattled. Every loose piece of metal sounded as if it might fall off somewhere along the road to town. My hair tangled with the swirling red dust as I held Daddy with a force I never knew I had. It was as if Daddy and I were one. I hoped he felt my strong, hopeful heartbeat. It was like a chant echoing my words: hold on, hold on, hold on.

Through the dust, I saw a pale day moon rising over the trees in the east. The hot sun beat down on Daddy and me as mile after mile the bumpy roads led closer to help. But would we be in time? Finally, on the edge of town, we flew past the cemetery, past small tumbledown houses built on brick pillars, and past yard dogs that stood up quickly and watched the truck zip by too fast to chase.

I could barely see the top of Celia's head; she sat so far forward, scooched down to reach the gas pedal, the clutch and the brake. She made a wide pitching turn onto Main Street, blazing past the gas station where men sat visiting and drinking soda pop. The owner, Jack, raised a hand to wave, but when he saw Celia and me in the truck, he took off running behind us.

Celia drove straight through the single stop sign on Main and pulled sharply toward the east side of the street down the block from Lewis's saloon, not stopping until she was in front of Dr. Haas's office. She clutched and braked so hard that she completely disappeared from my view.

The squealing and screeching brought everyone out to the street to gawk at us.

Dr. Haas was in the truck bed in seconds and unclasped my fierce grip on Daddy's bloody body. He worked frantically over Daddy and yelled orders to the curious bystanders to step back. He called to his nurse to hurry and call the ambulance and the hospital over in the county seat.

But people gathered around anyway, staring at us: two young blood-covered girls. When I saw Elmer run across the street from the Farmers and Merchants' Bank, tears streamed down my dirt-covered face, mixing with the blood that covered me, then staining Elmer's shirt as he kneeled and pulled us to him, taking charge.

Suddenly, Celia jerked away, as if awakening from a faraway place. She whispered, "Elmer, you know Mama won't like us to be seen like this, dirty, in front of people. We're supposed to put our best face forward."

"It's all right, girls, I think you have," Elmer said.

"But no one is supposed to know our troubles," I sobbed.

Celia hugged me close, then told Elmer where Mama and Sarah had gone.

Elmer hurried us across the street into the bank

until the ambulance arrived, sirens wailing. Then he ran back, helping Dr. Haas and others move Daddy onto a gurney into the ambulance. As it roared away, Elmer got some keys from his desk and motioned us toward a sedan parked nearby.

As we climbed into the back seat, Celia protested, "But I can't just leave the truck."

Elmer explained, "I made arrangements with Jack from the station. The truck will be fine. I'm taking you home—we'll wait for your mama there."

We huddled on the rear floorboard, not wanting to get blood or dirt on Elmer's car seats. As we drove off leaving the crowd behind, I began to shake. Celia took my hands. She whispered, "You were brave." Nodding, I bit my bottom lip and laid my head on her shoulder.

When we reached the end of Main, Elmer turned right, headed back past the small houses and the cemetery and onto the dirt roads, retracing the long miles we had just traveled.

Once in the countryside, I was glad when Elmer began to speak. "When I was a young boy, I heard grownups and kids talking about how Arley Poynter was the best ballplayer anyone ever saw. They said he was going to be like Babe Ruth, and his fans loved him. Some people nicknamed him Doak. When I first saw him play, I couldn't believe how spectacular he was. Every young boy wanted to be just like him. I did, too. Your Daddy was the most gifted and popular player anyone around here had ever seen. I heard he'd had humble beginnings and that endeared him to his fans. I believe he represented a dream of greatness for ordinary people in a desperate time.

"During those hard years most people faced long odds, but they thought: Arley made it, maybe I could, too." Elmer said over and over, "Girls, don't worry, he'll be alright—he has it in him, he has that something special."

Celia and I just looked at one another, even though what Elmer was saying made me want to smile with pride at Daddy's reputation. But I knew Elmer had not seen the bull spinning and spinning—with Daddy hooked on Old Hitler's giant horn. Elmer had not watched him fighting to breathe, silent and unmoving on the long, bumpy road to town. Daddy had stayed tough, he never once whimpered. I looked at my bloody clothes, my legs and hands—shaking hands that had held him so tight, not wanting to let go. He's too strong to whimper, I thought. I closed my eyes and said a little prayer. "Dear Lord—make him the Daddy we once knew. Make him strong like he was when he played ball."

Nearing the lane to our house, Elmer slowed the car. "Well, girls, will you look at that." There was Teddy, still sitting in the middle of the red dirt road. Waiting.

***

We all sat on the porch steps, Celia, Elmer, me, and Teddy, watching for the red Chevy. When it finally came down the lane, we were both at Mama's door before the car came to a complete stop. Mama heard only snippets, "Old Hitler," "the truck," "hospital." Our red-rimmed eyes and Elmer's presence revealed more than any words.

Mama shushed us, hugging each of us, touching my red-dirt, tangled hair. She said, "We need to go a little slower—one at a time. Let Elmer begin."

"Well, I'm sorry to say, the girls have had a terrifying day. The bull gored Arley, and unbelievably, they saved his life," Elmer said.

At Elmer's words, I gripped Mama, searching her eyes and wishing I could have prevented the day's disaster. "It's a miracle they could get him from the bullpen and into the truck. Then to drive it on into town." He shook his head. "Remarkable." He went on. "When we got back here, and while they cleaned themselves as much as they could, I checked the bullpen. It's clear the goring was grim. Arley lost a lot of blood. He was unconscious when they reached Dr. Haas's office, but he still had a heartbeat."

Mama sucked air deep inside her chest—gasping.

Quick tears stung my eyes. "He held on, Mama," I added quickly. "And I did too. I held him tight."

Celia shook her head, crying again. "Daddy was

wild mean, Mama, and I said a lot of hateful words I wish I hadn't."

Elmer put an arm around Celia's shuddering shoulders and took my hand, his solemn blue eyes sought Mama's. "These are the bravest girls I've ever known. They're strong like Arley. He'll pull through." Squatting between us, he said, "Don't forget what I told you today, and know this: He can't die. He has an unfinished game to win."

As the sky turned purple and dusk began closing in, Mama folded Celia and me in her arms leading us to the house, leaving Elmer and Mr. Harris behind.

Once inside the dim kitchen, Mama fell into Daddy's rocker, cupping her face in her hands.

She murmured, "Lord Almighty, I hope Elmer's right—that Daddy will make it."

Then, almost to herself, "Oh Arley, I'm sick at heart over you." Whispering, "All these years, me hoping you'd find your way, get your grit back. But you let me down. And now this."

She rocked back and forth, eyes closed, like she was praying, or thinking, maybe. I heard the summer locusts calling as dusk turned to night. We lit no lamps. We did not move. We stayed perfectly still as Mama rocked and rocked and rocked.

Suddenly, she stopped and turned to us, "He's hurting you now—all his turmoil and fear—it's too much."

Then she struck the rocker arm so hard I jumped. "Why can't you beat your damn demons, Arley?" Celia began crying, so Mama quickly added, "Now, don't worry girls, maybe when he heals, he'll be different. It's best to keep believing." She choked on the words. Struggling. "We've got each other, and you know we won't give up."

Then she crumbled. For the first time in my life, I watched Mama break down. Grief came tumbling out. She bawled like a baby, shaking her head from side to side, using the hem of her dress to dry her face, wet with her own tears.

It sounded like her heart just broke into little pieces.

TWELVE

WE HAD A FITFUL NIGHT. Celia slept in the middle between Sarah and Mama in the big bed next to mine. Sarah calmed Celia when she cried, and whenever Celia cried, Mama cried. We were exhausted. But bit by bit Celia and I shared what happened. I could barely stand reliving it all.

I'd forgotten all about April. He must be hungry! But Mama said, "He'll be waiting for you in the morning. Let's rest, girls—and try to sleep. We'll need all our wits and every ounce of energy tomorrow."

I woke early, climbed from my little bed and hurried to the barn. There was April, waiting, just as Mama had said, and glad for food and a hug. I was feeding him when I heard an engine and rushed back through the barn door, in time to see Elmer's sedan and Mr. Harris's shiny Chevy turn into the lane. I ran as fast as I could to the front porch, where Mama and my sisters gathered in the early morning sunlight.

Elmer's downcast eyes and furrowed brow frightened me. When we went into the kitchen, I saw him glancing at the burned linoleum flooring in the corner where black streaks still glared though fresh paint. He noticed me watching him and did his best to give me a quick little smile.

He said, "Arley is in very serious condition—critical condition. Dr. Haas called before sunup, Lou, and asked if I would drive you over to the county hospital as soon as possible."

Sarah came to Celia and me, taking our hands to calm us. Mama hesitated, then shook her head. "What about the girls?"

Mr. Harris saw her worry. "Lou, your sister Polly wants the girls at her place. I can take them over there. And, you know that Robert, my hired hand, and I'll watch over this place. We'll do the chores." He looked straight at me, he managed his funny little chuckling noise and offered, "I'll even take care of April myself!"

I pulled free from Sarah and ran all the way to the barn and April. I could see Daddy spinning and spinning, his eyes full of fear, pain all across his face. I kept trying to believe that since he never whimpered, never screamed, he must not be hurt that bad. But in my heart, I knew he was. All that blood. I wished and prayed for a miracle.

I was bawling into April's curly red hair, his halter bell jangling, when I felt someone's presence. I glanced up and saw the blurred outlines of Celia, with Elmer looming behind. Celia knelt and hugged me, saying over and over, "It's my fault, my mean words."

It was then we heard Elmer's soft voice. "I need to tell you two something," Both of us looked up at him.

"You are the bravest girls anyone could ever know. None of this is your fault. It was an accident. It was a terrible accident. You are amazing girls, and your Mama needs to see how strong you are right now. We need to hurry, and we must have a plan. Let's go," he said. "You help your mama. I'll help your dad." And on the way to the house, he explained some things we could do.

As Mr. Harris drove along the rough roads to Aunt Polly's, I couldn't help thinking that Elmer might be the best friend Daddy ever had, and Daddy didn't even know it. Of course, Elmer had been my best friend first. Somehow, he'd felt our incredible need and when he'd heard the kids' hurtful words, he'd reached out, not just to me, but to my sisters too, all kind and natural-like. Rumors told he had seen terrible things in the war and even I knew sissies did not receive medals. Whatever the reason, he knew how to react in a tight spot, and his belief in us gave me the courage to go forward. In some strange way, Elmer had become a part of our struggle. Like Mr. Harris, he seemed bound to our lives.

When we arrived at Aunt Polly's farm, she and Uncle Albert and their girls, Janie and Carolyn, streamed out of their hilltop house, hugging us to them, then gathering the meager belongings we'd hastily thrown into a cardboard box.

"Is this all you brought?" Aunt Polly asked Sarah.

Sarah stood looking at the box, "We may not be here very long, Aunt Polly. We're hoping Daddy will be okay and we can get back home." Then she added, "Thank you for having us— we'll help you—Mama said you're into canning from your big garden."

Aunt Polly clapped her hands and laughed. "You bet you can help! Janie and Carolyn are excited you're here. They're sick of picking tomatoes!"

At first, it felt like Aunt Polly glossed over the concerns we had for Daddy. She pulled us into their everyday life, keeping us occupied and more than a little bit tired.

"Once we finish with the tomatoes, we'll gather field corn," Aunt Polly announced like it was a game.

And as Aunt Polly's heavy pressure cooker steamed, spat, and rumbled on her huge cookstove, we spent hours cutting and preparing the vegetables for the glass Mason jars.

As the days passed, we worked constantly, helping with the meals and other chores. When it was my turn to gather eggs, it made me miss Mama even more. Sometimes Janie and Carolyn wanted to play Annie Over or catch fireflies, but I was so worried, I couldn't see the fun of it.

In the evenings, I just sat with Sarah or Celia, and when Aunt Polly played the piano, I grew sad and missed Mama even more. Why hadn't she telephoned? It must be because there was bad news, I thought, very bad news.

When there was free time, I roamed aimlessly, often climbing the shade trees nearest the road to watch for Mama and news of Daddy. But, as the long days passed, Mama didn't come. And never telephoned.

Aunt Polly tried cheering us up saying, "No news is good news. It's best not to worry so, girls—and don't forget how strong your mama is."

"Daddy's strong, too. He's not one bit Indian, like Mama, but he's just as strong," I said.

Aunt Polly frowned.

"Aren't you Indian too, Aunt Polly? We heard the Indian clan story during the reunion. Do you know which clan we belong to?"

"What clan story?" she asked, searching our faces for a clue. Janie and Carolyn giggled and grinned at me as I repeated the tribe lore. "Cousin Philip told us that there are seven clans in the Cherokee Tribe: Bird, Paint, Deer, Wolf, Blue, Long Hair, and Wild Potato. We think Grandpa and Great-Grandmother Caroline, and all of us, must belong to the Wild Potato Clan. There's your cousin, Tater, and we almost always only eat potatoes."

At that, Aunt Polly gave out a war whoop then laughed loud and long, but she didn't declare a clan. Even I joined the fun, but as the days dragged on with no news, the same sadness settled on me again.

Our supper conversations became more strained. Aunt Polly and Uncle Albert never even talked about Daddy or what might happen. What if he died? Celia and I became more desperate, confiding our fears only to one another. One night after days of worrying, we decided to talk to Sarah. She was in the parlor hand-sewing on a dress.

Celia approached her. "It must be awful news if Mama won't tell us anything. What will happen to us, Sarah?" She continued, her words coming fast, "If he dies, how will we live? Even if we could pay off the government loan, no bank would loan money to a woman—for land. There's almost no way Mama can earn money."

"Mama can't teach school. All she knows is farming," I said. "Sarah, what will we do?"

Sarah drew us to her. "Now, stop this talk. You know Mama would say that we'll find a way through this mess. She'd say we'll do the best we can. That's all any of us can do. You know we're really good workers, and don't forget: We must. We can. We will. So, whenever you get nervous, just say that over and over—and believe it. Besides, Mr. Thurston is a good man; he'll help us, I'm sure." She pointed her needle and thread at each of us, "Daddy will make it. Remember what Mr. Harris said when he drove us over here."

We grinned at one another. "Daddy is as tough as a mule."

*

**

Weeks later, I wandered alone near the barn. Hearing the cheep-cheeping noise of what Mama always called the "back to school" bugs made me homesick. I longed to see Mama and Daddy and Teddy, and especially April. As I roamed, I spotted Uncle Albert's truck turning into the driveway. He saw me and yelled, "Come to the house, and hurry!"

Did he have news of Daddy and Mama? I ran up the steps into the kitchen, just as he unfolded a week-old county newspaper on the tabletop. He was grinning. I edged closer to the table as Sarah, Celia, Aunt Polly, and the cousins gathered around him.

I couldn't believe my eyes. On the front page were two large photographs. One was of Celia and me walking toward a car. The other photo was of Daddy and a dark-skinned man in baseball uniforms smiling broadly. The headlines read, QUICK THINKING GIRLS SAVE DAD. Underneath, I read, "DOAK" POYNTER IN CRITICAL CONDITION.

"Oh, no—critical. It says *critical*," I said, grabbing Celia's hand.

Sarah read the article aloud. It included the details of the bull goring Daddy and spoke of the courageous efforts of his daughters. It mentioned that Celia could barely see over the dashboard and how they'd had to pry me from Daddy.

As Sarah read, it even told of how as a young man nicknamed Doak, Daddy had been a star—and how he and the other man in the photo, Tom Ausbie, were thrilling to watch. But then he had given up the game. I listened to the words as they now urged Daddy to win this game of life or death for his brave girls.

There was no mention of whiskey. I breathed a sigh of relief. Daddy's drinking problem lay hidden between the lines.

Celia and I read the paper over and over whispering to each other about our photograph and about Nola's article probably being a part of Elmer's plan to help Daddy find himself and his pride.

I was almost too excited to eat supper. I was picking at my food when I heard a car approaching.

"Well, wonder who's out at this time of evening?" Aunt Polly asked.

Tires crunched the gravel, as whoever it was turned into the driveway.

Peering from the window, Aunt Polly announced, "It's Lou, girls. Your mama's here at last."

Suddenly, it was chaos! We screeched as we scraped our chairs back from the table.

She was smiling. I thought she looked more tired than I had ever seen her, but she was smiling. She had to have good news, I thought. When the hugging, kissing, and greeting ended, I noticed Elmer leaning on the fender of the car. Celia and I ran, begging him to come into the house for supper, too.

Once at the table, I asked, "Tell about Daddy, quick, Mama, tell us!"

Mama began, "The doctor said if Arley had been ten minutes later getting to the hospital, he would have died." She added, "He said Old Hitler's horn just missed a major artery. He was torn up terribly. He has really struggled, and it took several doctors to put him back together. I've been so worried. It has been touch and go. But he's going to make it. It will take a long time to mend, but he's going to survive."

She smiled at us, and pulled us to her, "No one can believe two little girls could save his life, but you did."

Celia looked at her. "I just kept telling myself I could drive that truck. I knew I had to."

I chimed in. "We just pulled together, Mama, like you tell us to do. We're tougher than you think. I may be small, but I am strong, too!"

With that, everyone laughed, and Uncle Albert asked, "Let's see those muscles, Maggie."

I bent my arms at the elbow, revealing what any twelve-year-old boy would love to claim.

Elmer smiled right at me. "Your Daddy has received an awful lot of mail ever since the newspaper story. You gals are big news. Doak's old fans are writing to cheer him on. Looks like he's found a little spark from his past."

I smiled at Elmer and he winked. He was behind the photographs and the article. I was sure of it.

Mama nodded, "Daddy can't believe he has so many friends. The cards are so inspiring." She reached out and squeezed my hand.

Mama was so full of hope. She seemed almost happy. Daddy must have found his grit. Maybe the worst was over.

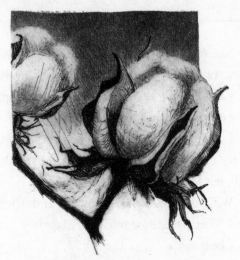

THIRTEEN

BY THE TIME WE GOT home from Aunt Polly's, the buttery-yellow full moon was cresting the horizon. Teddy jumped off the porch, running around in circles in the car lights he was so excited to see us. He romped around, jumping up on each of us. I'd never seen him so happy.

When Mama and Sarah scooted into the dark house to light the lamps, Celia and I hung back with Elmer, quizzing him.

"How will Daddy be whenever he comes home?" Celia asked.

I chimed in, avoiding Elmer's eyes. "Is he going to be Doak again? You know, I've been praying for that—like you said—Daddy's so strong, he could be Doak again."

Elmer chuckled, took my hand, and patted Celia's shoulder. "I can't promise you that, but I think he'd like to be good for you all. Especially for your Mama. Like I told you, we're doing everything to help him. He's getting a lot of mail, but a letter from you girls would be the best. Tell him what you're doing and hoping?"

"We will; we'll write tomorrow," we promised as we watched Elmer climb into his car.

I stared at the road until the taillights went over Johnson's hill thinking about how lucky we were to have such a great and helpful friend.

The next morning when I heard the early birds chirping in the lone catalpa tree, I jumped from my little bed and threw on some overalls to hurry to the barn where Mama and Celia were already milking. I knew April was waiting for me!

In the kitchen, Sarah stopped me, saying, "Remember Mama said we all have serious work to do—and you cannot just roam around with April while the rest of us do what needs to be done. You shouldn't be so attached, and anyway, how can you care for any bull after what happened to Daddy?"

I ignored her and went straight to April's pen. Once he was fed, I fastened his lead and tugged him, ringing his tiny halter bell all the way to the creek. I'd missed our long walks. I kept my arm around his thick curly neck. I knew he couldn't stay tame and sweet forever.

Nature wouldn't allow a bull calf to remain so calm or allow himself to be harnessed, but I loved him so much. My fear of losing him grew with every step.

We made a quick turn near the creek before returning to the barn. I watched the yellow streaks in the east sky widen, coming together in a blush high on the roadside cedars before I locked April up in his pen again. Even though it was as hot as the Fourth of July, the sunrise and the crickets' loud chatter signaled fall. I wondered what it would bring to us and the farm.

Just then, Teddy's barking announced an unexpected arrival. Suddenly about a dozen Negro men and women appeared in the distance. They must have walked the long way from town. Carrying their folded canvas sacks, they were turning into the lane. They marched along, forming a semicircle around a smiling giant of a man. He appeared to know Mama well. "Howdy do, Mrs. Lou," he called to her, folding her name inside an infectious laugh.

He walked over to us girls, stuck out his hand, and announced, "I'm Tom Ausbie, the guy in the newspaper picture with your dad." He squatted down next to me. "Doak and me are old friends. You know, some men have a tough time, no money, not much schooling, just born-in talent. Your dad was like that—started life like that—we grew up a lot alike. We didn't have a thing but baseball. Then we threw that away, too."

He glanced at Mama as he continued, "Anyhow, Doak got a good woman and three fine girls. He don't realize it, but folks still think the world of him. He's a good man, always helped me out.

"One time he brought Dr. Haas himself to save my sick boy—and more'n once he got me from trouble with the law," he chuckled, "I guess he'd give me the shirt off his back, if I needed it. And every cotton time, he's been generous and fair to all of us who walked here this morning."

"Hell," he said standing quickly, "we all against hard odds now and then. Ol' Doak, he just regret his losses more than some do." Then looking at the pickers, he said, "We came here to help him and you gals get that cotton picked, and we're gonna do it in a hurry, too."

The pickers clapped as Mama hugged Tom. Then she smiled and suggested, "Maybe you all could camp out down by the creek until the crop is in? It would save you the long trip back and forth to town."

Tom turned to the group, "That way we could be in the field before sunup when it's cooler."

They nodded in agreement. In fact, I didn't think they were surprised at all about the camp plan. Maybe it was Elmer's idea to help us out, or maybe they really did like Daddy so much they wanted to do it.

Mama smiled. "Girls, let's help set up the camp. Sarah, bring skillets and a soup pot. Maggie and Celia, gather eggs and some garden vegetables and lots of cellar potatoes. Tom, you'll need to move firewood from the pile near the chicken house. I'll get quilts once we make some beds of barn hay. There will be plenty of milk and food for all!"

Building the campsite was exciting. I was glad to do something to help. When Mama and Sarah brought plates and utensils to the rock-rimmed cook fire, I wished I could stay too. It felt like the times we kids played house at Grandma Judy-Bob's, pretending to make imaginary rooms under the trees.

Even though everyone helped prepare the site, it took about half of the first day. While we worked, it was decided that Tom and a couple of others would do the milking and other evening chores, so that whenever the wagon was full of cotton, Mama and Celia would pull it with the tractor to the gin in town.

The first afternoon of picking began ceremoniously as Celia and Tom hitched the tall-railed cotton wagon behind the rumbling Allis-Chalmers tractor. I scooted up the rails into the empty wagon for the ride west beyond the farmhouse. As Celia climbed aboard, she stopped, giving me a knowing look, before she sat straight and tall on the tractor seat, just as she had on that awful day.

I turned from watching Celia just in time to see Mr. Harris arrive. He greeted Tom like an old friend, grinning and shaking his big hand. It was the first time

I'd seen Mr. Harris smile since before the war telegram arrived telling him of Daniel's death. I studied the
two men and suspected that Tom's arrival was for sure
another part of Mr. Harris and Elmer's plan.

*
**

The days had been a blur ever since the pickers' arrival.
Each morning, Mama and Celia joined the field hands
working the long rows side by side, just the way Daddy
did before the accident. Dragging their long canvas
sacks, the workers called back and forth to one another.
Despite the hard work, they laughed and sang songs as
pretty as the fluffy white cotton they pulled from the
black bolls.

In the kitchen, Sarah and I prepared the noon meal
of green beans, boiled potatoes, sliced tomatoes, and
buttered homemade bread. My main job was to fill glass
Mason jars at the water well, loading them in a small
wooden dolly-wagon to pull to the field. Teddy stayed
busy running between the house, the field, and the barnyard, where an unhappy April bellowed, locked up in his
small pen.

Each day, under a makeshift tent stretched to one
side of the cotton wagon, Sarah spread a colorful ironed
tablecloth and laid lunch on a rickety table.

Tom signaled the sun was at midday by whistling

long and loud. The workers made their way, joking and teasing, to the wagon. If their sack was full, they'd drag it along for Tom to weigh on the cotton scale hanging off the rear of the tall wagon. Sarah recorded the sack's weight in her ledger, then the picker would dump the cotton into the wagon. Each person had his or her own page in the ledger book so that each time they weighed their sack Sarah would tally the number of pounds that person had picked and would pay each the money earned per pound.

As the wagon filled, Tom and some others would climb into the cotton and tromp it down tight, so the load would make a full bale in the ginning process. I loved scampering to the top rail to watch their dancing feet. I couldn't resist jumping down into the cloudlike softness myself, gathering armloads of the white cotton and shaping it into imaginary chairs, stools, and a chubby bull calf that looked a lot like April.

Some of the pickers came up with a competition to see who could pick the most cotton in one day or who could fill their sack the fastest.

The betting contests were settled with Lucky Strike cigarettes, although some of the men rolled their own. I watched them pour loose tobacco from a pouch onto small white squares of thin paper, then roll and lick the paper shut. It became an odd-shaped stick to smoke. It seemed to me that Tom encouraged the happy mood, not only to lift the workers' spirits, but ours as well.

We wrote letters to Daddy with news of the harvest and funny tales from Tom's camp that would lift his spirit, too. Sarah helped Celia and me find the right words. We struggled to soften exactly how we felt. We knew we couldn't mention the accident. We didn't like reliving it ourselves and we didn't know what he might be feeling. Instead, we told about how big April was and how Teddy had worn a path running back and forth to the pickers. We told him how much fun Tom was. How he joked and pranked us. We knew how terrible Daddy must feel. He had worked night and day to grow and harvest this cotton, without it we'd lose the farm, and now he was missing the harvest altogether. I wished he could see how hard we were all working for him—and for ourselves—so we could keep this place.

Every few days Mr. Harris appeared, sometimes riding Midnight, his black horse, right into the field to speak with Mama and Tom. His picking crew was busy, too. I heard him say, "The cotton is coming out of the fields in our county fast. Wilbur, at the gin, is one happy man. There are long lines of trailers overflowing with cotton. It's a great harvest. That cyclone just hopscotched across the county, missing most of the fields. Then he paused. "Lou, I saw Mr. Thurston yesterday, he said he's coming to talk to you this week."

I cringed. Did Mr. Thurston have bad news for us? He had been so encouraging when he was here the last time, but that was before the storm hit our field.

One evening before dusk, Sarah and I carried a warm blackberry cobbler and pot of coffee to the workers' campsite. The aroma of camp food cooked over an open fire hung along the creek. I liked to visit the camp. The women pickers were fond of me, fooling with my blonde curls and teasing me to make me laugh. I heard Tom doing his best to cheer up Sarah by bragging about her record-keeping and calculating skills to the others. Even I had seen how she was patient, showing each person the numbers for what they had picked and earned so far. But, still, she seemed distant. Sad.

Tom must have sensed her sadness too, for he encouraged Sarah, "This is good quality cotton and despite the storm, the yield is big. Everybody knows Doak gets more bales to the acre than anyone in the county. For sure, gal, this is gonna bring good money for you all, never a doubt."

Long after dark, beyond the campfire shimmering in the trees by the creek, I saw the headlights of the tractor topping Johnson's hill. When the buzz of the engine pulled into the lane, the moonlight illuminated Mama and Celia's straw hats.

"Well, you'll never believe it," Mama said, removing her hat and shoes. "I suppose we're simply the talk of the town. Tonight, Wilbur came back in the line and said for us to pass to the front of all the wagons. He said from now on, we're always to go ahead of all the other wagons. He persuaded the others to let the ladies go first."

Celia imitated Wilbur's deep voice, "A lone woman and three girls working night and day to bring in a harvest. I never heard of such a thing!" Celia laughed, "I guess he's never heard that Mama can outwork two big men. The farmers all tipped their hats to Mama and me and we pulled right inside the building and onto the gin scales to weigh the wagon. This guy gets into the wagon and with a hose sucks the cotton into a real noisy machine. I learned it takes six hundred pounds to make a single bale of cotton. Wilbur said we've got a lot of bales so far!"

I grinned. "Tom said we're going to get a lot of money!"

Mama added, "We're ahead of Tom's estimate. He's right, this is a very good crop, but don't get your hopes up. It most likely won't bring as much money as we need." Then she added cautiously, "We've got a long way to go before we know for sure. Don't count your chickens before they hatch. I'm tired, girls; let's get some rest. The sun gets up early."

*
**

A few days later I saw Mr. Thurston, in his government car, pull into the lane. Elmer's car was right behind. And while I was cheered by the sight of Elmer, I stood frozen. What would Mr. Thurston tell us?

As Mr. Thurston opened the door, he spotted me and smiled. "Hello, Maggie! Lost any more teeth?"

I grinned despite my worries.

Then Elmer chimed in, "I hear you're quite a ball player—like your dad, I guess."

That made me feel proud as I ran ahead to lead them to the farthest west field.

Seeing the two of them, Mama flushed with embarrassment at her shabby appearance, then she stood, adjusting her hat, regaining her composure. Walking between them, she began detailing the harvest, and I followed nearby, hoping to overhear. Both men were intent on Mama's words. "The yield is as good as Arley ever had," she said. "This is the healthiest cotton, and the bolls are the fullest I've ever seen. But you can see the toll of the storm throughout the fields. I am uncertain of our volume. It's going to be short, I'm afraid.

I'm trying to be realistic." Gesturing with her scratched sunburned arms and bleeding hands, she somehow still seemed optimistic.

I stayed as near as I dared, suddenly overhearing "Daniel" and "Harrises' barn." When Elmer called out to me, I jumped, startled by his sudden attention.

"I saw your daddy yesterday. He sent a letter. It's in my car." Elmer grinned, his blue eyes motioning me to follow. "I think he's finding his way, Maggie." His warm hand on my shoulder was enough to make me believe it might be true.

*
**

In the days after, we read and reread that letter until the paper grew limp. I especially liked the part about the accident where he said,

> I am so lucky to have you smart and strong girls, no one can believe how brave you both are! I will try to straighten up and stop the crazy things I did, I promise. Lots of people wrote letters caring about all of us. I know I have hurt you girls and your Mama, but I will work to regain your faith and confidence. I've been fighting to recover, and I am winning. I've had many visits and help from Elmer and Mr. Harris, too. They've both talked

a blue streak about how proud they are of each of
you. I'm proud, too. I'm so sorry I will not be able
to come home in time for Daniel Harris's funeral.
At least I get to come home someday soon.

Daddy

P. S. Lou, tell Tom thanks for hitting a "homer"
in the fields and for being a good friend.

We kept the letter in the top drawer of the buffet.
Sometimes Celia and I took turns reading it aloud when
we were in the house without Sarah and Mama. Could
it be true?

"Do you believe it, Celia?"

"Some of the promises sound pretty fancy, like
how he's winning and straightening up."

"Maybe Elmer helped him find the words. He said
Daddy's getting better."

"Maybe so. I want to believe it, too," Celia said.
Then her face clouded over. "But I'm afraid he won't
keep to these words."

She folded the paper and stuck it back in the drawer.

"I hope you're wrong," I fretted.

"Well, he's coming home. I guess we'll find out."

FOURTEEN

THE DAY ELMER AND MR. THURSTON came to check on the cotton harvest and Elmer hand-delivered Daddy's letter, Elmer also surprised us with a fully charged battery for our radio.

I'd jumped up and down, but it was Sarah who said, "This is better than Christmas. We haven't heard music or the news in a long time. Thanks, Elmer!" I couldn't help smiling as I thought, even Sarah's getting comfortable with Elmer's help.

In this morning's frenzy of baking and ironing, we had been elated to hear President Truman announce that the war with Japan was officially over! I wondered if the atomic bomb had been the reason.

I watched Mama sink into the rocker and sigh. "Oh my, I'm happy and sad at the same time," she said. "Lordy mercy, this will be a difficult day. Daniel's funeral on the very day of the war ending will be emotional for everyone, but especially for Mr. Harris."

A few hours later, Mama drove down the lane and navigated carefully among the parked cars and trucks surrounding the Harrises' golden-yellow farmhouse. We saw Mrs. Hopkins and Mrs. Loper from school, Reverend Perkins from the Baptist church, and neighbor ladies fussing over covered dishes spread on plank-topped sawhorses beside the long back porch.

Seeing the big crowd, I couldn't help wondering, what if it were Daddy's funeral and no one came? He had closed himself off from almost everyone. But, still, I knew if he were healthy, he'd be here today for Mr. Harris. Daddy and Daniel had been friends.

At the bottom of the hill, Mama parked our truck near the huge barn and next to a black hearse. Tom and five other pickers crawled out of the truck bed and walked over to Elmer, who waited at the open barn doors.

Mama steered us inside the great barn. Hay bales formed pewlike rows in the vaulted middle section and wooden folding chairs were lined under the wing lofts.

Mama gripped my shoulder when she saw the casket on the far wall opposite the entry doors. I saw it then, too. I'd never seen a casket. It was boxlike and was wrapped in the American flag. The stars and stripes were almost shining in the dark barn. Standing beside it was our country's flag and the blue state flag of Oklahoma. I could see the image of the Indian shield on it, and I looked for the eagle feathers that represented the tribes of Oklahoma hidden in the folds.

Nearby, two uniformed soldiers stood at attention, their eyes locked on an invisible spot over our heads. Colorful ribbons decorated their jackets.

I knew this ceremony was important, and I took it all in. But I had an uneasy feeling, and I felt lonesome even though I was sitting right next to Mama. The war had always seemed so far away, but it was right here today.

As the crowd filed into the barn, Celia elbowed me when Nola placed a vase of zinnias beside Daniel's casket. She peered about, finally choosing a chair near us.

In the stillness, a horse whinnied. Slanting rays of sunlight fell across the enormous space.

At last, Mr. Harris, Ruby, and Nadeen crossed the space and sat in straight-back kitchen chairs near the casket. Elmer followed, in full military uniform, also decorated with ribbons and shiny medals. He saluted the flag and turned to face the crowd.

He began, "During these long years of war, in small towns like ours all across the country, heroes have died for us. I believe as long as we do not forget their sacrifice, they will not be lost to us forever. Soldiers like Daniel went to war because it was too important not to. We have all been caught up in the effort to win this war. Remember when President Roosevelt said, 'the determination of the people will triumph, so help us God!' We mourn that neither Daniel Harris nor FDR will hear the news of victory this day. We salute Daniel's courage, his faith, and selfless perseverance in the face of battle. We are thankful that his life served freedom." Elmer paused briefly, then continued, "President Harry Truman sent Daniel's family this message."

> In grateful memory of Daniel D. Harris, who died in the service of his country. Daniel stands in the unbroken line of patriots who have dared to die that freedom might live and grow and increase its blessings. Freedom lives, and through it, he lives—in a way that humbles the undertakings of most men.

He added, "Mr. Harris and Daniel's sisters' lives will never be the same and neither will ours. Daniel was a hero for each of us. Keep him in your hearts."

As Elmer moved to stand beside the two soldiers, one of them stepped forward and presented Mr. Harris with the fringed gold star banner usually presented to

Gold Star Mothers for a son killed in action. Mr. Harris clutched it, great sobs shaking his frail shoulders. I saw Nadeen and Ruby look at Mama, their eyes pleading for a hand to hold onto. Mama went to them and held them close. Suddenly I realized Daniel would never see his family again, never hug his Daddy, never get to drive his red Chevrolet. Never know he'd been his Daddy's pride and joy. I was sick at heart and started to cry. Sarah pulled me close, putting an arm around me.

From the loft above came voices. The voices of Tom and his crew filled the barn with song, a spiritual so full of harmony and power that the mourning crowd stood to sing with them.

> Swing low sweet chariot,
> Coming for to carry me home—
> A band of angels comin' after me,
> Comin' for to carry me home—

I was too sad to join in, even when everyone sang "God Bless America."

But it was Elmer's words at the end of the service that moved me the most "Each of us must have courage—and stay strong—and *be more for others.*"

Sarah suddenly turned to Celia, whispering, "Be more for others. That's it! That's why he's helping us. The war made him someone who wants to help others."

I looked at Sarah. "Celia and I've known that ever since Daddy's accident."

Celia nodded. "Remember how he bragged on Daddy on the way home from town? He didn't want us to give up."

Sarah hugged us both. "Well, I admire him. He's sure been good to us, and Mr. Harris has been, too."

We left the barn, walking with Tom and his crew, praising their singing.

The neighbor women were busy serving a bountiful feast. I found Mama and stuck beside her while Celia and Sarah went to sit with Ruby and Nadeen to help them get through this: their only brother's funeral.

Then, Mama and I carried heaping plates to Tom and the others where they waited and watched from the bed of our truck. Mr. Harris, too, carried a large platter and shook their hands, thanking them for the beautiful music.

Later, several neighbor men approached Mama and me to ask about Daddy and inquire about the progress in our fields. I noticed some women gesture toward us, whispering behind their hands. There it is again, I thought. Nola's newspaper story has got the tongues wagging.

I was proud of Mama. She was beautiful and businesslike, and told the men, "We've got about two weeks left at the most."

The men all agreed the harvest was nearly done. Mr. Wilson, our neighbor, suggested, "It's a good idea to send your pickers in a sweep back across the fields to pick any late opening bolls. It all adds up."

As I listened, I thought the men questioning Mama on the cotton was odd. It sounded like they thought she might not have enough cotton and were getting her ready for disappointment. One thing I knew for certain, if Daddy were here, they wouldn't be questioning him. I couldn't help smiling. They just didn't know Mama.

When the crowd began to thin, Robert, Mr. Harris's hired hand, led Daniel's sorrel horse, Buck, up the hill. Buck was saddled, and ribbons and tiny paper flags were braided into his long silky mane.

As Nadeen stroked Buck's neck, she turned to Celia and me, then sighed. "Papa said Buck has to lead Daniel home."

As afternoon shadows fell across the cedar lane, Mr. Harris, riding Buck, led the hearse on its sad journey. Elmer climbed into Daniel's red Chevy with Ruby, Nadeen, and Robert and followed. We joined the slow procession in our rickety truck as neighbors, in a cluster of worn-out vehicles, followed the winding road to the tall iron gates of the cemetery where townspeople stood waiting.

FIFTEEN

DANIEL'S BURIAL DAY STRETCHED PAST sundown. In the dim light of a single oil lamp, we sat looking at one another in silence.

Then Sarah finally spoke. "I couldn't believe how many people were waiting in respect, and how when Mr. Harris touched his hat brim, like a salute, sitting tall and proud on Buck, it was so sad. It meant goodbye, I think."

"Oh, yes," Celia said, "Wasn't Buck grand standing right on top of the burial dirt, the breeze ruffling his mane and the little flags?"

"It was sure kind of Elmer to help with Buck when all those people crowded close," Sarah added. "It's good Mr. Harris has Elmer and Daddy for friends now. Elmer was a rock for him today."

"He's kind of a rock for us, too. How do you think Elmer and Mr. Harris connected?" Celia asked.

I sat next to Mama, dragging my fork through my leftover peas.

"I think the sting of war connected them and then Daddy's accident gave them both a purpose, something positive to work on together that had nothing to do with the war," Mama said.

Sarah looked straight at Mama. "They've both been amazed by your grit, Mama, and they must believe Daddy's worth rescuing. They have big hearts, and I think they really care for us."

I nodded, thinking of Elmer when he brought us home from town after Daddy's accident and told us not to worry. I thought, everyone likes Elmer, but I love him the most.

"They are unusual men. They are wise and decent and folks respect that," Mama said. "Elmer is idealistic, and Mr. Harris is commonsense."

I moved onto Mama's lap.

"What is idealistic?" I asked.

Sarah said, "Elmer wants everything to be as perfect as it can be."

"But Mr. Harris has lived longer and knows that life isn't always perfect. He is down-to-earth and always has been," Mama said. "Right before you were born, Maggie, the first day Daddy and I met him, he recognized that your Daddy was trying to overcome something—something big. He could see Daddy was strong but had little confidence, yet appeared hungry for a new chance. I kind of thought Mr. Harris needed something, too. He seemed lonely."

Mama stared into the lamplight as though she was reliving it all again. "I remember that day so well. After we signed the rent papers in town, we came out here to see what we were up against. The place was in shambles, and Daddy and I were standing in the overgrown grass near the windmill wondering where to start when Mr. Harris rode down the lane on the biggest black horse you ever saw. He really must love black horses best. He circled around, sizing us up. Then he asked, 'You folks planning to live here?'"

"We nodded, and he told us about the family who'd scraped out a life here for fifty years before the bank foreclosed on them. Their people had settled this very land in the Territorial Land Rush of 1889, when you could stake a claim and actually own the soil.

"'They gave up,' he told us. They just gave up on their home, their land, themselves. He guessed the dust carried them out west, maybe to California like so many other Okies. The last time he saw them, their belongings were crammed into two worn-out pickups. Two men and some kids were waiting around the trucks for a lone woman to come from the house. Before she got in the truck, she looked at Mr. Harris and pointed to the open door and announced, 'We never had a key and, anyway, now the place is free of us. Let this awful dirt and dust take it back.' He said he would never forget her tired, forlorn face."

Mama paused. "On that first day we met, Mr. Harris stared at the empty house a long time before he said the place had been free of anyone living in it for many years. Said he'd kept the doors shut and watched over it some."

"Everything was rundown, deserted. Dirty. I remember how surprised we were when he said it was fate he'd ridden by that day. He looked your Daddy square in the eye and said, 'Son, this is a good piece of land, I'll bet you can make something happen here. I'll help you.'"

Mama nodded, recalling, "He reached out and shook Arley's hand that day and he has never let go."

Then looking down at her own scratched and calloused hands, she sighed. "Oh, we were plucky then."

SIXTEEN

THE LONG HOT DAYS DRAGGED by before another wagonload was ready for the gin. Tom asked to ride along so he could check on his family and the other workers' families in town. He said, "I need to buy some cigarettes and tobacco too. I'll keep you all company."

Celia urged, "Maggie, you and Sarah come too. You can meet Wilbur."

Mama added, "Yes, we'll all go, and Sarah you can check your numbers against the gin's records. We'll celebrate the almost end of cotton."

I was tickled to death to have a trip to town! Tom, Sarah, and I rode in the wagon on top of the sweet-smelling cotton, laughing at Tom's antics and attempts at joking. He fell asleep about halfway along the bumpy road. "He's just worn-out," I said. We woke him when we arrived at the gin yard.

Tom climbed down the side rails, "I won't be long," he said, hurrying from the wagon. "I'll meet you right back here."

"Cotton season must almost be over," Celia remarked, looking around as if she was an expert. "Only one wagon is in line for the scale. Come on, Maggie, I'll show you the machinery while they deal with the numbers."

When we came out of the gin, we heard Mama arguing with Wilbur. Sarah stood beside Mama holding the cotton ledger in her folded arms, her eyes blazing.

I heard Wilbur say, "I'm sorry, Mrs. Poynter, I have to hold back money for two bales for Boots. He showed me a paper Doak signed to pay his whiskey debt at the Blue Moon. Boots warned me if I didn't give him the money, there'd be hell to pay. I know how you feel, but I'm in the middle and no one messes with Boots, not even Doak. Not even you, Mrs. Poynter."

I had never seen Mama this angry and defiant. Her face was red, her black eyes wide, she was slapping her hands together and her disheveled hair was falling from her bonnet. "This cannot be true," she announced, then ordered us into the empty wagon. She pulled out of the gin yard and drove the tractor toward Main Street.

The town was rolled up tight. The stores were closed. Dr. Haas's office was dark. I saw a single light shining in Elmer's bank, but there was no movement on the street. We huddled in a corner of the wagon as Mama crossed Main, heading into the Negro neighborhood.

"She's going to the Blue Moon," Sarah half-cried over the noise of the tractor.

"Stop her, Sarah!" begged Celia. "Boots is mean. Fierce mean."

Night was falling, the dusk thin, as the tractor lights inched closer to the Saloon.

Mama pulled the wagon to the side of the street across from the Blue Moon, where the bright colors of neon beer signs and the jukebox beckoned through the window.

Sarah and Celia hunkered low near the front of the wagon. When Mama killed the engine, Sarah begged, "Mama, this is not the thing to do. Let's go home. You know he's a bad person. He won't listen to you."

"Stay in the wagon," Mama ordered. She threw her bonnet on the tractor seat and turned toward the lights and the open door.

In the darkness, I slipped from the rear tailgate and crept behind her, scurrying into a small space behind the open glass door.

I saw that the place was empty, except for a hefty

Negro man behind the bar. He looked up in surprise at Mama.

"Boots, look at me and then take a good look out that window at my girls in that wagon. We worked hard for our cotton, and we got it out. It is not your cotton; it is not your money. I don't know if Arley owes you or not, but I do know you won't get this cotton money, not now and not ever, not this cotton money. You have no right to tell Wilbur to hold our money back for you," Mama declared.

Boots raised his hands in a gesture of nonchalance and drawled, "Sorry, Mrs. Poynter, Doak done gave his word and signed over two bales. Doak, he hurt now, but he gonna get hurt worse if you don't pay the money. It's due. Hell, woman, it's way past due. Two-three years past due."

I saw Mama tighten her jaw. "No, never!" she said.

Boots nodded his head and said, "I'm sure times is tough for you. It's tough all around. You'll pay all right." Laughing, he added, "You already paying. Everyone say you always save Doak. You never quit on ol'-good-fer-nothing-but-whiskey Doak." Taunting Mama, he raised a bottle in jest.

I watched in amazement as Mama rushed toward the bar, arm raised as if to strike against his ridicule and laughter.

Boots took her wrist and pushed her toward the far

wall. I saw him reach below the counter, just as Elmer and Wilbur burst through the open door. "Wait a minute here. What's all this noise and fuss about?" said Elmer.

From my vantage point, I suddenly spied Tom stepping through the rear alley door. Moving into the narrow room, Tom glared at Boots. "You rob Doak and don't care who you hurt, but you're not going to hurt Mrs. Poynter and her girls. You're not. I'll not let you."

Through the dirty glass door, I watched Boots's anger grow. His fierce eyes locked on Mama, then Elmer and Wilbur on the far wall. He slid his arm above the counter, and the neon beer lights glittered on the pistol in his right hand.

Elmer cautioned, "Tom, slow down."

But Tom moved faster toward Boots who shifted his focus away from Mama, yelling, "You just love your old Doak, don'cha, Tom? You nothing but a whitey-lovin', washed-up ballplayer."

Tom jumped over the bar, grabbing Boots's right arm, struggling over the gun. Mama and Wilbur dropped to the floor, but Elmer rushed to the scuffle. I heard bottles breaking as the men lurched, pushing each other trying to gain hold of the pistol.

There was a quick snap, followed by two popping noises. Then there was a cease of movement and a release in the scramble of men.

"Oh my God," Tom whispered as I watched Elmer fall to the floor. Boots stood still, holding the gun, surrounded by silence.

Suddenly, Sarah and Celia rushed past me. As Wilbur and Mama scrambled to their feet, Mama spotted me behind the open glass door. I pushed through them. I had to get to Elmer! Mama tried to stop me, but I broke free. Shaking at the sight of the red blood spilling on his white shirt, I called his name over and over. I clutched his hand and leaned close, but his eyes were unseeing. "You'll be all right, you're okay, look at me, Elmer!" But he didn't move. "Look, Elmer, it's me, Maggie," I begged. "Please look!"

In the chaos, everyone was yelling and crying, but Mama stood tall and commanded Wilbur and Sarah to run for the sheriff and Dr. Haas and Nola, as Boots slunk out the rear alley door.

Then Mama rushed to me and Elmer. "Tom, help me find his heartbeat. Please, oh please, God." They kneeled, working around us, trying to find some sign.

I watched as the revolving lights of the silent jukebox spread an eerie rainbow of color in the dark corner. Shivering, I clung to Elmer's hand, as I whispered his name over and over, hoping he'd hear me.

Many voices, familiar voices, echoed dreamlike around me, until I heard Dr. Haas say, "Maggie, I'm here now." He stepped over me and Elmer, interrupting my vigil. I recognized Nola's scratchy voice asking questions. I heard footsteps banging out to the alley. The quick snap snap of the rear screen door sounded like shots. I jumped, then stood, shaking, afraid Elmer was gone forever. "I need Elmer, Mama. We all need him. Please, Mama!"

Mama pulled me into her arms. She was talking, trying to make sense where none existed. I drew away from her and saw her eyes—sad and scared.

Finally, she carried me outside, where Sarah and Celia sat on the edge of the porch, sobbing.

They came to us and formed a tight circle, their strong arms holding me. Mama rocked us, murmuring, "Be still, we must all be still now."

We heard Tom humming, then his grand voice cracking and breaking, as he slowly sang, "A band of angels comin' after me, comin' for to carry me home." Then—I knew.

Elmer's battle for good was ended, not at bloody Omaha Beach, but in a dirty saloon in his beloved hometown.

SEVENTEEN

I LAY AWAKE MOST OF the night. I kept seeing Elmer's motionless face. I could still smell the whiskey, hear the gunshots, and see the colorful jukebox lights rotating inside the Blue Moon.

When sleep came, I dreamed of Daddy and Elmer. They were shadowy, faint, just out of reach. Daddy told about quitting things and how he always lost people he loved, like his brother, Bill. He said, "When Bill died, I started drinking whiskey to forget—I'm always losing the things I love most."

As Elmer took Daddy's hand, he came into focus, becoming bright, almost sunny—his whispery voice floating like a song, "Arley, don't quit. Don't quit your girls. Winning is your legacy, not losing."

I woke up with a start. I was sweating and blinking, hoping to see Daddy and Elmer again. They were gone. All I could hear was Mama weeping in her bed next to mine. My dream was so clear. I saw Daddy's blue eyes and Elmer's, too. And I'd heard Elmer's words.

I'd become used to Daddy being gone. After the bull goring, I'd even thought it was kind of a relief to have him gone. We didn't have the whiskey worry threatening us, waiting to cause more unhappiness. But I'd kept hoping our dreams would come true. Now, I wasn't sure.

Suddenly, I felt cold and was shaking again. Elmer was gone—really gone. I wished I'd told him how much he'd meant to me. I hoped he knew.

Before sunup I heard Mr. Harris arrive. My heart pounded, then I heard a chair scrape and coffee cups clinking. I crept down the steps and sat at the bottom of the stairs, watching through a crack in the door, trying to overhear their words. It appeared as if Mama was blaming herself, her nervous hands and shaking head moved continuously. Mr. Harris stared into his cup, weeping softly and wiping his eyes with his handkerchief.

She began to pace, trying to explain the unexplainable. "Why someone as good as Elmer would be killed will be an unanswered question forever." Raising her arms as if in defense, she added, "It was senseless, and Boots will pay now."

Suddenly, Sarah scooped me in her arms and pushed through the door into the kitchen. Mama stopped pacing. She sobbed at the sight of us.

"Things would be different if I hadn't gone to the Blue Moon," she said, crying aloud. "Girls, you know I'm a fighter like my grandma. I never want to give up. I didn't see the danger. I believed I was right, and I went to the Blue Moon to make Boots see that. But I was wrong, so wrong."

Sarah glowered. "You were furious, Mama, and you wouldn't listen to us. If only Wilbur hadn't run for Elmer. He must have known Elmer was our friend. They must have come to help us with Boots." She paused, then continued, "And, really, it's Daddy's fault too."

Celia, now perched on my stove bench, joined in, "We shouldn't have gone there. Elmer got shot over Daddy's problems. Daddy should've fought his own fight."

I saw Mama's discomfort. She was searching for our understanding. Then she crumpled into a chair, "Oh God, forgive me for taking Elmer's help. I should have noticed he was too involved. I should have seen a warning."

Mr. Harris, tears streaming down his cheeks, watched Mama, then he nodded, dabbing his face. "I'm trying to understand, Lou. But coming so soon after losing Daniel is more than I can bear." He sobbed. "Elmer's been my strength lately, helping me look ahead—but I swear, I can't see any future today!"

He stood, holding his hat in both hands, and spoke directly to Mama, "We'll need to go tell Arley."

✳✳

I spent the next few days in the field near Tom. He let me ride on his cotton sack, pulling me along the rows behind him, like Daddy used to. Tom saw my despair. When the pickers' songs and gospels made me cry, he'd whistle and everyone would go silent, their heavy snake-like sacks swishing up and down the rows.

He encouraged me, "Things gonna be okay, Maggie. Doak gonna come home. He gonna be right as rain for you girls."

But Tom never spoke of Elmer. He didn't have to. I knew he felt as terrible as Mama. As terrible as we all did.

Several mornings later, Mama mentioned, "I think it's best if just Mr. Harris and I go to Elmer's funeral."

"No, Mama, no! Elmer was our friend. We cared about him so much and he cared for us!" I said in disbelief.

Sarah agreed, "It's true. It's because of us he grew to care about Daddy and you. We need to say goodbye.

192

And think about Maggie, Mama; Maggie will never have any peace if she can't find a way to understand this. Even though she saw it happen, she can't accept it. She needs to say goodbye more than any of us. You know she was his favorite girl in the world. They had a kinship all their own."

Trying to hold back tears, I stood up. "Elmer told Celia and me to be strong and have courage. I have to go—to show I'm strong, to show I care."

Celia joined in. "We have to face this. And we must face the townspeople, too. Everyone knows our troubles now. There's not much left for people to say anyway."

We watched Mama. She roamed the floor in our silence.

Finally, she spoke. "I've long been defending Daddy and his weakness, protecting him until he found strength and willpower again. I've cared because of love, not just for him, but also for you. I know what you're thinking. If Daddy hadn't had the debt with Boots, things would be different, or if I hadn't gone into the Blue Moon or if Tom or Elmer hadn't come, or . . ." she paused.

"I think you should know Daddy is grieving terribly over losing Elmer. He feels guilty, too. But, I will still be for him whether he is right or wrong. We're all struggling now. And we're at a place where we must give up or push on past this. It happened, and it's awful.

"I thought you should not go to the funeral because people might say hurtful things. I was trying to keep you from feeling what I feel—utter failure," she said.

Sarah spoke up. "We can't pretend it didn't happen. Whatever is said will not change us. Like you've always told us, we'll keep on going, and we're going to get through this together."

How was Sarah so smart? It seemed as if she was older—older even at times than Mama. It was clear to me that Mama was led by her heart and Sarah by her head.

Mama looked at each of us. "You're right. We should let people see how much you cared for Elmer. We should be proud he cared for us. We should all be there for him."

*⁎
*

The gothic white frame Methodist church rose above a sea of people. Sadness engulfed the community; black mourning wreaths hung on shop doors and houses.

Mr. Harris, Mama, and us girls pushed a path through the crowd toward the steps. People murmured and stared. I gripped Mama's hand, scarcely looking above the feet of the people we passed. I was not afraid, but anxious and lonesome for something I couldn't explain. It was in the pit of my stomach, an ache of longing and sadness. I followed Mama into a pew, laying my head against her side, as the minister began the eulogy.

He spoke of Elmer's life and love of others, of his selflessness and sacrifice, of his heroism during war and even here and of now being at peace. He spoke of Elmer's love of children and how he put others first. He told of miracles and unexplained losses in the world.

All the while, I closed my eyes, picturing Elmer's wink in the bus rearview mirror and his electric smile.

When the service ended, we traveled for the second time in just the space of a few weeks to the tall cemetery gates, red dust rising behind the cars and trucks.

Tears streamed from our flushed faces and Mama's too, as the final scripture was spoken at the graveside. Mr. Harris leaned on Mama like a crutch.

I watched Elmer's mother rise from her chair beneath the burial tent, working her way through the throng toward Mama and us. I glanced up at Mama. Her fingers found my hand. When Elmer's mother reached our side, she opened her arms to envelop us and we hugged like family.

"Elmer admired your girls ever so much, Ms. Poynter. They were a bright spot in his life. After he was wounded and came home from the war, he was despondent and withdrawn. But once he started driving the bus, he was different. He began to perk up, to look ahead again."

She studied each of our faces. "He spoke of you girls so often I feel like I know you." Her faded blue eyes looked first at Sarah then Celia and me, as if she was memorizing every feature. Instantly, I took her hand in mine. Searching her face, I finally found the words and I whispered how much Elmer had meant to me.

"Elmer was my best friend. Maybe could I be your friend? I could come see you or you could come see me and my calf at our farm. Did Elmer tell you we've been working to keep our farm? Did you know he was helping us? He and Mr. Harris had a plan. They're very good friends, too," I said, pointing to Mr. Harris. I suddenly stopped talking, then fell into Elmer's mother's arms.

In the days after, we went about our lives, silent, trying to adjust to this horrible truth. The pain of Elmer's loss was too deep. Too deep for words.

During the last of the cotton nights, I heard Mama crying again. And I could hear my sisters talking in the dark, trying to find a way past this hard place. In the mornings, Mama's face was swollen, her eyes and nose red. She sighed loud heaving sighs, as if she might be taking her last breath. One morning she confessed, "I have so much guilt. It was not right to covet this farm so much. I was rash and desperate. I just wanted our own home.

I'd give anything I hadn't gone to the Blue Moon. I'll always blame myself. I was too eager to get this place."

I looked up at her, "Elmer thought we should try to get this farm, too. He said our plan was the right thing to do. Remember, he told Celia and me to help you and he'd help Daddy. He and Mr. Harris were better than family. They'd never want us to give up."

Sarah moved toward Mama. "You can't blame yourself for trying to resolve Daddy's problems. You were desperate for us." She paused. "You've always been strict with us—but weak with Daddy."

"Daddy's drinking changed us, even you, Mama. He tore apart our affection, scared us, and ripped up our life. He deceived us. Maybe now, if not for us, at least for Elmer, he will find his way. It seems everyone loves Daddy—and we'll have to try to forgive him, if we can, and love him again.

"But Mama, Maggie's right. We can't quit, with him or without him. Ever."

EIGHTEEN

IN THE PALE NEW DAWN of the last cotton day, I saw birds, hundreds of birds, filling the sky, soaring in an ever-changing pattern, heading south for winter. Sitting on the rail fence, I watched the milk cows trudging along their rutted path toward the barn, their fat sides wobbling, one behind the other. Teddy, ever loyal, was running the distance of their line, barking, urging them forward. The old bell-cow leading the way, her neck bell clanging with each step, reminded me of April and my dilemma.

Mama kept saying we needed every penny we could get to pay off the government loan and so I knew when the time for the cattle sale came, I'd need to let April go.

I'd have to, because I could, and it would be my way to help. I didn't know how, but I would find the courage.

The recent sad days had slipped away until today's quick sweep of the fields would top off the final wagon for the gin.

Late that afternoon as we broke down the worker's campsite, Mama told everyone, "As soon as Sarah settles your wages, we'll take you all home on the cotton wagon." Looking at each worker, she said, "I hope you know how grateful we are for your help. Thank you is not enough to say, not nearly enough," her voice breaking.

Then she turned to Tom, "You've been our angel in disguise." Her voice broke again, and everyone grew quiet. "We're going to miss you, Tom." Gathering herself, she smiled at the pickers and said, "Maybe, just maybe, with Arley's good cotton crop, we might still be on this land next year. Will you come back?"

The pickers clapped and climbed atop the soft cotton, carrying their folded canvas sacks and wearing the same ragged clothes they'd worn when they walked into our lives weeks ago.

As the wagon rolled, they began singing, first singing the songs we knew, and then breaking into spirituals of their own. Their harmony was wondrous. At the edge of town, people came out of their houses just to listen, and witness the sight.

Mama and Celia sat tall on the tractor seat, bonnets

back, hair streaming, pulling the wagon with me, Sarah, and the workers perched on the cotton all singing together. That, too, would soon be the talk of the town.

A full moon punched above the horizon, grazing the treetops as we approached the gin yard, where several wagons and tractors lined the entrance.

We saw Mr. Harris standing beside his big red Farmall tractor. Wilbur was there and curiously many other neighbors we knew. Even Uncle Albert. The men whistled when Celia shut off the engine, gathering behind Mr. Harris.

I was surprised to hear his odd little chuckle. Then he continued. "Well, we've all done another year of cotton. You know, cotton is a mean crop. Now, it's also a money crop, and a good one this year, but it takes a lot from people who work it. We've never seen anyone work cotton like you, Lou Poynter. You and your girls are special. Everyone here had promised Elmer their last wagon just for you gals—and for Arley, too. Elmer loved you all. He wanted to help make your dreams come true."

Hearing his words Mama buckled. Then she climbed down from the tractor shaking her head in disbelief. Mama shook hands all around, struggling to find the words to thank each farmer for his generosity. "Lordy mercy, I never heard of such kindness," she said, patting Mr. Harris's shoulder. Her loud sobs filled the quiet.

When Celia jumped from the tractor, Sarah and I scurried down the side of the wagon alongside our pickers.

Sarah and Celia said goodbye to them, but I stayed in the shadow of the wagon watching Tom and Mr. Harris talking apart from the group. I thought, it's just as I suspected, Tom was in on Elmer and Mr. Harris's plan all along. Tom saw me watching them and came to me saying, "See, gal, I told you everthing goin' to work out." Then he winked, and before I knew it, he and his enormous smile disappeared into the night.

The noise of the gin broke the quiet as Celia drove our wagon onto the scale; the suction hose cleaned the last of our good crop. We called goodbye, and in the light of the full moon, headed out.

Back at our lane, Teddy ran circles around the empty wagon and the Allis-Chalmers before Celia cut the engine. She and I then hurried to feed the mules, Old Hitler, and April.

At the supper table, everyone talked at once, excited about the day. Sarah asked, "How could Elmer, Mr. Harris, and our neighbors even think of such an unbelievable gift?"

Mama added, "It's uncommon—the idea of giving away their cotton—it's unheard of. Why they made up for our lost cotton! Oh Lordy, that Elmer, always helping solve our problems and Mr. Harris, too. I feel like my heart is breaking. I'll never get over it." Pausing a bit, she suddenly said, "You know, Daddy never believed in taking anything from anyone. Maybe now he'll see that folks learned from Elmer how to pull together and help others. He'll accept it."

I looked around the table. "I was thinking about Daniel's funeral when Elmer told us all 'We will never be the same.' Daddy won't be the same either. Elmer believed in Daddy and so do I. I think it was Elmer's plan, and Tom's too, for Daddy to be Doak again."

That night I lay awake until everyone seemed asleep. Then I scooted downstairs and got out my keepsake box that I'd hidden in the buffet. I plopped on the floor in the bright moonlight streaming through the kitchen window, then picked up my stubby red pencil, fingered my FDR pin, and found the black and white photograph of Daddy as Doak. For a long while I studied the picture of me and April in the flower bed that Sarah took last spring. April was so small then, and I was too. But we were both bigger now. Big enough to help.

NINETEEN

SCHOOL WOULD BEGIN SOON. I wasn't ready. I was worried about facing the kids on the bus, and especially, the new driver. And my fear of letting April go nagged at me. Since the cotton days had ended, I'd had too much time to think. How could I lose April too? What would I do without him? I fought my dread by walking with him in the pastures.

We set out before sunrise on the morning of the cattle sale. The clouds were thin and yellow, like the leaves in the north pasture trees. The wind ruffled April's curly red coat as we moved along a cow path. I felt a lonely feeling, sort of like homesickness. I kept telling April that I had to give him up, but that he would live on a different farm where some other kid would love him as much as I had. I knew I was just making believe that somehow he'd be spared. Suddenly, I cried out, hard and loud, causing the big bull-calf to stop and turn his eyes on me. When he jerked at the halter rope, I told myself, "He's ready to be free—like the others."

I felt guilty for being selfish. It hadn't been fair to April, to tame him and spoil him just for myself. Grandpa had tried to tell me, but in my uncertain world, April had been my one dependable thing. This had to change. I would face this new loss and overcome it. Somehow.

We approached the farmhouse through the garden, Teddy racing ahead, barking at the large cattle truck as it backed up to the loading ramp of the corral. Several men with long sticks began guiding the bawling calves and heifers onto the ramp. Mama stood next to Mr. Thurston, overseeing the head count.

As I tied April to his usual porch post, I heard an engine noise in the distance. I saw a small truck, followed by a long black car on the road. The truck quickly entered our lane, but the long black car stopped, letting the dust settle before finally turning into our lane, too.

I realized what it was. "It's Daddy!" An ambulance had brought Daddy home, on this day of all days. We gathered at the windmill, as Mama, smiling, ran up the hill. She looked so happy. For the most part, Daddy's absence had made it possible to lessen our fear of his reckless behavior, but here he was, home. How would he be now?

Two men opened the rear door of the ambulance and pulled the rolling stretcher forward. Teddy darted near, whining, circling, and echoing the wild mournful sound he'd made when Daddy was hurt by Old Hitler. Surprisingly, Daddy raised one hand toward him. Teddy jumped, licking it, wagging his tail in joy. I came unstuck and hurried toward Mama's laughter.

It was startling to see his face. His blue eyes, shiny and questioning, were accented by a dark red scar across his handsome forehead. He appeared happy and sad at the same time, but his pain showed clearly. He looked at each of us, searching our faces for anger or resentment—or love.

I moved forward and grasped his big hand. But Sarah and Celia remained motionless. Silent.

At Daddy's side, Mama said, "We'll put him in the spare bedroom off the kitchen, until he can walk again."

I waited beside the ambulance until they disappeared into the house, then I got April and went to find Mr. Thurston, who had finished counting the cattle. He was figuring in a notebook and turned. Suddenly, he put his hand on my shoulder. I thought, he knows.

I tried to keep calm, but my eyes were glassy and brimming full. "Mr. Thurston," my voice was small but steady, "I've been thinking for some time that my bull is too big for a pet. He's full grown now. He's twice as big as the others, and he's so smart. He must be worth a lot. Do we need more money?" Before I knew it, Mr. Thurston had reached down and gathered me in a hug, "Maggie, just like that, you've grown up. You've had the hardest summer. You are one remarkable girl."

I sobbed, then leaned heavily into Mr. Thurston's shoulder, trying to overcome my sorrow as one of Mr. Thurston's men took April's lead rope from my clenched hand and led him up the ramp into the truck. Mr. Thurston held me tight while I blubbered all the way to the rear screened porch.

We found Sarah and Celia preparing lunch, while Mama was settling Daddy into the spare room.

"Excuse me," Mr. Thurston spoke. Everyone glanced up as he moved me closer to the bedroom doorway. "It's good news, folks! It looks like the numbers are adding up to a bit more than what you owe the government. You would've been quite short without the extra cotton from the neighbors and if Maggie hadn't let the young bull go."

I watched Mama's face puzzle then her shoulders straighten. She rushed through the doorway. "April? You mean April?" she questioned.

Mr. Thurston looked at me. I nodded.

From the bedroom, I heard Daddy call out, "No! Take the mules instead of her calf. That calf is hers."

Mr. Thurston lifted a hand and said, "No one wants mules, Arley. Keep them."

I felt weak as Mama knelt at my feet and hugged me. She looked up at Mr. Thurston.

Mr. Thurston placed a hand on his chest and smiled at me, "Maggie did it herself. I would never have thought of it. It was her decision to let the young bull go. She's right; he'll bring a lot more money than your old bull."

I saw Sarah and Celia coming toward me. I stood tall, but I felt miserable, and the sight of Daddy's crushed and tearful face was too much.

I let the screen door slam behind me, and I raced past the barn, running all the way to the creek, falling at the sandy bank and digging in the wet dirt with my fingers. The sky was spinning, and my head was filled with the sound of bawling cattle and gears grinding, as both trucks left the lane, moving toward Johnson's hill. When the engine noise grew faint, emptiness filled the air. I felt as if something died inside.

I saw Mama walking toward me. She looked both troubled and weary.

When she neared, she stood looking at me. "You are the most courageous of us all. You have suffered more than anyone—losing Elmer, and now this."

Then Mama pulled me to her. "I want life to be easier for you girls. You know I've worried sick over every penny, but I never once thought to ask you to give up April . . . not ever.

I gently pushed away from Mama's grip. Standing alone in the dusky quiet, I shivered, like before, listening for the gentle bawl of a spring calf that would never come again.

TWENTY

THE ODOR OF YELLOW-DEAD grass and drying leaves marked the quiet mornings after the cattle sale. The weather had changed; a light frost had pushed the creek trees into color. The reds were redder and the yellow leaves brighter than ever before. I stood on the front porch a long time looking past the barn. I thought even the barn looked worn out, as if it, too, had aged from the summer's harshness.

Mama called from the door, "Maggie, come in before you go to the bus."

Daddy, on crutches, hobbled to his chair at the oak table. His blue eyes watery. "I need to talk about Elmer and what he did for me. For us."

I grabbed Sarah's hand and Celia moved close to my side.

"I miss him—like you do. I'm full of regret. I'll never get over his death at the Blue Moon." He shook his head, staring at the table. "When Elmer came to see me at the hospital, he always told stories about you girls—and you too, Lou. He really was crazy about all of you. He talked about the war too, how it was a nightmare and had made him an old man. He said you helped him feel young again."

"It's strange, but he told me I was in a war too—in a battle with myself—and I was losing. Elmer was wise beyond his years. He made me look at myself. I saw I was weak. Where once I had been brave, I'd become reckless. He said over and over, "Doak, pull up that strength and courage you used to have and whip whiskey.""

Daddy hesitated. "I've lost him. And now it feels like I may have lost you, too. I know I've hurt you, but if you girls will give me a chance like Elmer did, I promise I'll never let you down again."

I watched him. His smile pleading and widening until it was just like his smile in the black-and-white photograph. Elmer's Doak was coming back in living color.

I waited to see if he dropped his eyes from my steely gaze. He did not. I longed to believe him, and I could see how his heart ached for me to do just that. I realized I'd been holding my breath.

When Mama patted Daddy's shoulder, his eyes filled with tears. She took his hand and put it to her face. Then she turned to us.

"Girls, you know I depended on you to be brave this summer. And I'm sure proud you were. You were strong. I'm sure you'll be strong again this morning and the mornings to come without Elmer. Try to help each other on the bus."

On the porch, I heard Teddy calling us from the cedars. The road seemed long, but the air felt crisp, and bits of bright frost glittered in the thicket pulling us along. We arrived at our four corners early and the waiting made me anxious. I mumbled, "I feel awful, and I think I am going to be sick."

Sarah gathered me close and said, "Maggie, I feel awful too." Celia nodded.

"When we get on the bus, try to be brave."

We heard the engine top the hill and the gears slowing down to gather us up. I began clenching my hands and breathing hard . . . tears were coming fast. How would I ever climb onto the bus, Elmer's bus, without him there?

The door opened and an older man in a wide brimmed hat helloed over the noisy bus.

Sarah hurried up the steps first, then Celia. I waited below, hesitating. And then, looking up, I saw something shiny hanging from the rear-view mirror, moving in the breeze. I climbed up the steps and stood there. Then reached out to touch them. The dog tags. Just seeing them there, in their usual place, was a sign for me. I knew I would never see Elmer again, but in a way, just knowing these were still here made me feel that every morning he'd be here, too, reminding me to stay strong. I turned and found my sisters.

*
**

It was a strange day at school. I'd moved up an entire grade altogether! When I asked my teacher, Mrs. Shafer, about James, she told me that he'd moved away during the summer. I realized that everything had changed for me.

After school, when we approached our bus, the new driver handed candy to each of us kids. He was trying to be friendly, but he would never be my Elmer.

When we neared our four corners, I saw Teddy was waiting as usual. He was standing next to Mr. Harris beside the mailboxes. His red Chevy sedan was parked facing the direction of our farmhouse.

"Sarah, look, something's wrong! Why is he waiting here?" I asked.

We tumbled off the bus with Nadeen and Ruby, quizzing him, while Teddy jumped all around us.

Mr. Harris opened the car door. "I'm taking you gals home today. And put Teddy in the car, too. We need to hurry."

Without another word, we climbed in. Teddy was confused and tried to pull away, but Sarah and Celia picked him up, holding him until he knew it was safe.

We were puzzled and swapped worried glances. I leaned up over the front seat and said, "I like the car ride; it sure beats walking, but has something bad happened at our place?"

He gave his chuckling laugh and waved a hand in the air dismissing my question.

When he turned at our house, Mr. Harris tooted the horn several times, like a song. Mama rushed to the porch first. Daddy, struggling with his crutches, followed behind her.

We piled out of the car trailing Mr. Harris to the steps, surrounding him as he pulled a yellow manila envelope out of his pocket. His grin a mile wide, he began waving it above his head. "Well, if this isn't a grand day! This is what you have been working for. I've carried the paperwork to you from Mr. Thurston. You satisfied the government! These Farm Security papers are marked PAID IN FULL. And it looks like Mr. Hopkins at the bank has said okay for your farm loan. Yessiree, it's a great day!"

"Truly?" Mama gasped, reaching for the papers. We looked at one another, startled. Then, joy reigned! We jumped around like little children at Christmas. Mama joined us, holding hands and making a circle of hops and skips, everyone yelling at once. Mr. Harris was like another kid, slapping each of us on the back, and laughing. Daddy's piercing whistles rang above the ruckus, and Teddy stood barking his head off, while Nadeen and Ruby stood staring at our crazy scene.

When the jubilation calmed, Mama declared, "This is unbelievable. Just amazing." She added, "See girls, it's the gospel truth, you have to work hard and for a long time before you can claim a place of your own. Lord knows it'll take us years to pay the bank for the land, but we can do it."

She hugged us, "Our work paid off and so did your help, Mr. Harris. You kept us going and lifted us up again and again. We're ever grateful! I'm so happy I think we need to celebrate. Everybody come in and have some apple pie—I think it's still warm."

I hung back, dropping down on the porch steps with Teddy. I was sure glad that Mama was happy. She'd pulled off the first hurdle. She'd paid the government people and saved our reputation. It had been a group effort. But I was thinking the good news might not be so good. Would Daddy be up to it?

I was uncertain. I knew that to really own the land,

would take more than Mama's grit— and more than Elmer's help and Mr. Harris's kindness. It would take a Daddy with willpower and perseverance. And he'd need more than his good looks and smile to tame the whiskey and red dirt.

I gave Teddy a pat and stood to join the others. When I looked up, I saw Daddy waiting for me. He struggled with his crutches, then asked, "Maggie?" He fumbled in his pocket. I heard it before I saw it. April's halter bell and faded blue ribbon. I rushed to grasp it. Then I shook it gently, all the while staring at Daddy, questioning, how?

"Mr. Thurston helped me find it," he murmured. Then he reached out to me, patting my shoulder. "I am sad about April. I am so sorry. I had to find some way to thank you. To thank you for helping me." I was astounded. I looked away past the barn toward the spring creek where April and I had gone almost every day, and clutched April's bell. It took a while to break the silence.

Finally, I looked at Daddy. "I was just thinking that it'll be a long time until you can walk with us to the bus again."

"Maybe by spring," he said.

"It feels like old times having you here," I said, then paused, and stared straight at him. "I sure hope you'll be different than when you left. You made me scared and worried, ruining everything like you did. Then after you were hurt, we were torn up and struggling. Elmer found us and put us back together."

My words were racing now. "I was afraid you couldn't heal—couldn't change. But Elmer, he believed in you. So, I did too. *I never gave up on you.*"

He stood silent, looking past me toward the pasture, but I could tell he was listening. And despite the lump in my throat, I went on.

"When I lost Elmer," I paused, "I decided to be stronger than ever and tougher, too. I have thick skin over my scars now."

I swallowed hard. He was still silent, so I went on.

"I'm hoping we can make it through the hard times ahead. All of us. Have you found your courage and strength? Can we count on you, Daddy?"

He offered me his hand and leaned close to whisper, "Maggie, remember our old saying 'never a doubt'? I promise I won't quit you girls again. Never. Ever. Maggie. You can count on me."

My eyes met his. Then I took his hand. He squeezed my fingers. And as we moved to open the kitchen door, I heard singing. It was Sarah and Celia. They were singing Mama's favorite song about a blue moon turning to gold again. And for the first time, I thought, maybe, just maybe, it's possible.

AFTERWORD

For the rest of his life, Daddy never drank whiskey again—not even a drop. He kept his word. He had uncommon willpower.

We never owned the farm. We left on a cold November day when I was fourteen. Daddy didn't have farming in his blood. His real talent had been baseball. He found a new game in the oil fields.

He promised Mama a warm house in a different town, with enough land for a big garden.

Mama enjoyed being near her sisters and the Baptist church. She trained and became a nurse. At ninety-three, she still wore high heels to walk her beloved dog—as well as to garden. Her gardening heels were caked in red dirt.

In spite of, or probably because of, those rough, lean years near Crescent, we girls flourished. We were resilient, and determined, beyond all knowing. We kept our work ethic, excelling in college and beyond. We each left Oklahoma and Mama's red dirt dream to follow our own. "Like birds leaving the nest," she always said.

We flew far and wide, always owning Daddy's willpower and Mama's grit in the retelling of this—our—story. In their lives together, Mama and Daddy nearly starved, almost blew away with the dust, and battled a demon. They and we never gave up.

Never a Doubt

ACKNOWLEDGMENTS

Deep gratitude to the inestimable Melanie Kroupa, editor, agent, wise counselor, and advocate. Extraordinary acclaim for the most sensitive and talented artist, Kyle Hobratschk, whose genuine belief in this story created such compelling images of Maggie's world. I am happy that our unique friendship has brought our work to fruition. Thanks also to his father, Allen, whose knowledgeable and supportive words, recognizing the vivid truth of the story's time and place, buoyed me. I am thankful, too, to Peter Cameron, amazing author and teacher and key advisor for my story's future. Added acknowledgment to the Sirenland Writer's Conference leaders, Michael Maren, Dani Shapiro, and Hannah Tinti, whose encouragement meant so much. I am indebted to Will Evans, publisher, for such fierce energy, as well as Jill Meyers's eagle eyes and the Deep Vellum crew for their dedication and skill. Thanks, too, to Kay Carlson, Katherine Krueger, and T. J. Griffin for their support and goodwill. Recognition for the late Ann Connolly Henry, whose research contributed the Indian tribal clan names. A special appreciation to my sisters, Frances Macy and Gloria Adams, my first teachers, whose love and bond of sisterhood survived many trials. Thanks also to Robin Macy for prodding my effort and to Phil Macy for his recollections of Boots and the Blue Moon. To my dear children, Eric and Lucy, and grandchildren, Elizabeth and Stuart—without your love and steadfast support I might have given up innumerable times. Big nod to granddaughter Stella, whose enthusiastic interest and contributions I found helpful. My family's kinship to this story urged me to never doubt I could do it. And, always, I must acknowledge Stuart, my husband, partner, and tireless tech support provider, whose uncommon love and unwavering belief in me sustained my long efforts. I am grateful to him and humbled by our once-in-a-lifetime love story.